To

THERESA!

Maniac Gods

Rich Hawkins

Thanks for the help and
support! You've a legend!

Hope you enjoy the book.

SINISTER
HORROR
COMPANY

PRESENTS

MANIAC GODS

RICH HAWKINS

MANIAC GODS

Edited by Daniel Marc Chant & J. R. Park
Interior design by Daniel Marc Chant & J. R. Park
Cover design by Vincent Hunt

Published by The Sinister Horror Company

MANIAC GODS -- 1st ed.
ISBN: 978-1-912578-05-4

ACKNOWLEDGEMENTS

I'd like to thank my family and friends for supporting me in this weird struggle we call life. Shout outs go to Adam Nevill, David Moody, Gary McMahon, Gary Fry, Tim Curran, Philip Fracassi and H.P. Lovecraft for inspiring me through their great work (check out their books at all good online bookstores).

Also I'm much obliged to Dan and Justin at the Sinister Horror Company for publishing my insane scribblings and being genuine good guys.

Lastly, I say thank you to Adam Millard, who took a chance a few years back and published my first novel. I'm honoured to call him a fellow writer and a friend.

This book is dedicated to William Hawkins.

'Hope in reality is the worst of all evils because it prolongs the torments of man.'
– Friedrich Nietzsche

PART
ONE

PROLOGUE

PROLOGUE

The girl stood at her window, watching the rain in the night, and saw the thin man in white robes slump to his knees on the road outside. Within the shadows thrown by the streetlights, he put his hands to the bronze mask upon his face and bowed his head. She thought he was crying, and wondered what he was crying about in the middle of the road beyond the front garden of her mother's house.

She wiped condensation from the window, breathed softly through her nose to keep the glass clear, and wiped her damp hand on her opposite sleeve. Droplets pattered against the other side and ran in vertical trails down the glass, turning the street outside into abstract smudges and smears. The man became no more than a forlorn ghost waiting for her in the downpour and the keening wind.

The girl squinted, watched the man while her hands pinched at the edge of the windowsill and the walls of her bedroom creaked as cold draughts rushed through them. She was vaguely aware of the sound of her mother switching on the shower in the bathroom down the hallway.

Aside from the erratic trembling of his shoulders the man didn't move, and for a moment the girl thought he was merely a product of her imagination, an illusion in the rain, until he raised his head towards the window where she stood, and took his hands from his face and gestured for her to come outside to see him. She stepped back from the window, surprised at the warmth of his smile within the mask he wore.

The voice inside her head was gentle and friendly. It was the voice of a kindly grandfather who loved his children and would never hurt any of them. *Come outside, dear one. Come outside and be joyous with me in the rain.*

Her hands shaking at her sides, she turned away from the window and left the darkness of her bedroom, passing into the pale light of the landing. She stepped quietly past the door to Mum's bedroom and went downstairs. The man's voice was in the wind, circling the house, low and wordless but comforting.

Pulling on her coat, she opened the front door and stood at the threshold as rain lashed the doorway around her. She squinted against the building storm. She swallowed, felt her throat working, and looked out at the man in the street. She couldn't stop the brief smile that curved her mouth.

The man spoke inside her head again, warm and honeyed, encouraging her forward, and she complied and left the house to walk down the garden path. She went out to him, leaving behind the shelter of the house. The rain on her shoulders, on her head, and then on her face when she looked up at the sheer black sky.

She shivered in the cold and stopped before the man in the road, returning the smile he gave to her. Their proximity revealed the full vision of his bronze mask.

She told him her name.

The man held out his hands and looked down at them, the smile fading from beneath his wet mask, his eyes glassy with sudden confusion and something like awe. Then he looked up at the girl and told her to come closer. And when she did, he put his dripping hands to her face, and she felt such warmth from his touch that she began to cry.

The man spoke to her, said her name, and comforted her. The rain went away and there was nothing but the warmth.

She only screamed once when the man's hands reached inside her head and found her thoughts and little dreams.

I

CHAPTER ONE

Albie Samways woke from a restless sleep on the sofa and remembered fragments of troubling dreams. He screwed up his face at the sour taste in his mouth and the nausea in his throat. Rubbed his stinging eyes until they felt better. There were three empty cans of cider and two discarded crisp packets on the coffee table. The air of the living room smelled stale, with a low mustiness in the corners.

He squinted and turned away from the overhead light, which seemed overly bright and glaring. His head thumped from dehydration and the sudden spike of adrenaline that had hit him upon waking. The television was muted, showing some old film he remembered but couldn't name. Something about planes and trains, he thought. There was only the sound of heavy rain falling upon the house.

He picked up his phone to check the time, saw it was near midnight and that he'd missed three calls from Kathleen while he'd been asleep. The last call had been thirty minutes ago. Shaking his head and stifling a yawn, he deleted the notifications until he came to the icon for a new voicemail. He checked the number. Kathleen, again. He exhaled, scratched his face, considered ignoring the voicemail, until he realised that people only usually call late at night when they've got bad news to share, and his face suddenly flushed hot and panicky with concern over Milly's safety. The separation from his daughter over the last year had only made him worry more about her wellbeing. She was prone to nightmares and sleepwalking.

Albie dialled the voicemail service, put the phone on loudspeaker, and waited. His hands weren't entirely steady as he listened. A muscle twitched beneath the skin of his face.

The voice message began with three bursts of static, spaced evenly apart, followed by a low whine and then something like a jumble of distant, slowed-down voices that seemed barely human. Guttural half-words and grunted barks that Albie couldn't discern. The faint screech of some animal heard from far away, blended with sounds like radio waves reflecting off the ionosphere and fragments of lost transmissions in barely-heard choruses. The slamming of doors. The snatch of a boy's voice singing a sad song while dogs barked and bayed.

Albie's eyes watered and the back of his hands and neck prickled. He swallowed to produce some saliva in his dry mouth.

The voices continued for several seconds before they were cut off by what sounded like the clumsy knocks and bangs of the phone being moved around. Then there was just ambient noise. He thought he heard quick footfalls in the background. He held the phone closer to his ear, and when Kathleen's voice rose from the silence, all slow and unfocused like she'd taken a heavy dose of medication, he could only sit and listen, one hand at his face, his mouth open.

'Albie, listen to me. Albie, listen.' Her voice dropped away, lost in a sound of rushing wind, and then returned again. *'It is open. It is all open in the thin places, and there is nothing to be done...'*

The message ended immediately afterwards.

Albie returned the call and waited, but no one answered, and on his fifth attempt the line went dead and that was that.

II

CHAPTER TWO

He pulled on his boots and thick coat and went out into the rain, leaving the lights on in the house. He locked the front door and climbed into his car, trying to keep a lid on the panic in his chest. Acid frothed in his stomach and made him feel weak and insubstantial, like an ageing puppet on thinning strings. The hurried walk from the door to the driveway had left him soaked and dripping. His breath was mist in the close confines inside the car. The rain scattered against the windows, a constant rattle, muffling the thoughts in his head.

He turned up the demister to remove the condensation from the windscreen, and moved the heater dial to red. He flicked on the headlights. The engine started on the second attempt and he took the car onto the road, putting his foot down and moving through the gears until he passed beyond the speed limit.

He'd considered calling the police, but a nagging thought told him he'd be wasting their time because probably Kathleen had just drunk too much, and it would be embarrassing for everyone involved. Not to mention that he was over the legal alcohol limit to drive himself. He kept telling himself that Milly had put her mum to bed and everything was all right. Milly was a good girl and knew how to deal with Kathleen's rare relapses. Most likely no one had answered his calls because Kathleen had put her phone on silent after calling him. It was the simplest explanation, and he clung to it and tried not to think of anything else.

And he repeated it in his mind, to comfort himself during the long drive to his ex-wife and daughter, while the rain grew heavier and obscured everything but the few metres of road ahead of him.

X

He drove for over two hours, from Somerset into Hampshire, and by the time he'd reached the outskirts of Penbrook his eyes were aching and the back of his legs burned with cramps. A dull pain pulsed behind his forehead. The rain had been continuous all the way down here, pushed by the harsh winds that swept across the roads, and even now as he entered the north edge of Penbrook he kept his hands tight upon the steering wheel as the car was jostled and pushed. He steered around occasional potholes and cars parked at the roadsides.

He'd only noticed the lights on in the first house moments after he'd passed it, and was surprised that someone was still awake. A factory worker recently home from a night shift, maybe, or just some night owl like himself.

But as he went deeper into the village, he saw that lights were glowing from windows in most of the houses he passed. The flickering of pale radiance from televisions in living rooms. He tried to glimpse any movement or activity within the houses, but it was difficult to do when he had to keep his eyes on the wet road and the rain.

While taking a bend in the road, he almost swiped the side of a Vauxhall Corsa parked clumsily at the kerb.

The streets were deserted. The overhead streetlights seemed to dim.

As he neared the village pub, which was lit from within, he slowed the car to a crawl and craned his neck to see through the front window of the building. And in those few seconds all he saw were empty seats at the bar and the jittery lights of a fruit machine.

He kept driving.

III

CHAPTER THREE

Albie stopped the car outside Kathleen's house and killed the engine. In the sound of falling rain upon the roof, he took a moment to slow his breathing and wipe the beads of sweat from his forehead. He exhaled through his teeth and prepared himself. Winced at the broiling of digestive juices and cider dregs in his gut.

It was always hard coming back here, now that this place wasn't his home and he was supposed to stay away except when he came to pick up Milly for their weekends together. A tremor passed through his hands when he took them from the steering wheel. He looked around at the houses veiled behind the downpour and the dark. The lights in the windows did not waver.

He hesitated before leaving the car, and then walked towards the house. He cringed in the rain as he opened the garden gate and took the path that bisected the lawn. Kathleen's car was on the driveway. The lights were on in the kitchen at the front of the house, and in Milly's bedroom directly above it, a lamp issued its soft glow; the curtains in the window were drawn open, and he half-expected to see her peering out at him, but she wasn't there.

The front door was ajar, letting rain into the house.

He hesitated again, swallowing the unpleasant knot in his throat, shifting on his feet as he laid a nervous hand on the door and slowly pushed it open.

'Kathleen?' His voice was flat and meagre in the rain. The darkness pressed at his back, and a feeling of being watched from the street behind him couldn't be denied. 'Milly? Anyone home? Hello?'

When no one answered he stepped through the doorway and into the kitchen. A sense of bittersweet nostalgia made his heart wince. So many memories. Good times and bad times.

He was careful not to slip on the rainwater pooling on the linoleum. He looked around, blinking rapidly, suppressing the urge to cough, and listening for any sounds in the house. But all he could hear was the constant rattle of rainfall and the creaking of the walls.

He was alone in the kitchen. All the doors on the wall cabinets were hanging open, showing boxes of cereal, a loaf of bread, packets of biscuits, multipacks of crisps and snacks. A Tupperware pot of rice and one of pasta. Cans of soft drinks. The appliances on the worktops were in place and untouched. Everything was in order.

He eyed a framed photo of Kathleen and Milly taken at a theme park two months before he and Kathleen had separated. He'd been cut out of the picture.

There were more photos, but he didn't look at them.

X

He searched the downstairs rooms, but there was no sign of Kathleen or Milly. He looked out into the back garden and found it empty. The only sign of any disturbance in the house was an ornament that'd been knocked onto the carpet in the living room. He picked it up and put it back on the mantelpiece above the gas fire.

He climbed the stairs to the narrow landing and announced his presence to anyone waiting for him in the rooms. A little voice in the back of his head scolded him for not taking a sharp knife from the kitchen. His feet scuffed on the carpet. The house made low sounds. Pipes scraped in the walls. The central heating switched on with a vague ticking.

In Milly's room he looked around at the posters of pop singers and film stars on the walls. Her teddy bear, which she'd had since her first day in the world and kept for sentimental reasons, lay upon her bed with dull eyes and splayed limbs. The room smelled of his daughter, and he kept expecting her to appear out of thin air and tell him there had been some terrible misunderstanding. He said her name to the silence.

The bathroom was empty and all in order, pristine surfaces gleaming from the new lightbulbs overhead.

In Kathleen's room, he found her mobile phone broken into several pieces on the bed they used to share. For a moment there was a vague taint of what could have been ammonia in the air, but it went away and then all he could smell was the damp reek of his clothes. By then he was panicking and his breath seemed to thicken in his throat and tighten within his chest. He leaned against the wall to steady himself as he called their names again and again, until his voice grew coarse and his eyes watered.

Then he went back through the house and searched once more, breathing hard and trembling, dazed with exasperation and confusion. There was no sign of a hurried departure, or even *any* sort of departure, like they'd just walked outside into the rain and left the house behind. Their coats were still on wall hooks by the front door. Nothing made sense.

Albie returned outside, hoisting the hood of his coat over his head, and hurried to Norris Witt's house next door. The rain was incessant and spat at his face as it was pulled by the wind. Thunder crackled in the middle distance, the sound of shifting mountains.

The lights were on in Norris's house. Albie knocked on the door and waited, then knocked again. After a few minutes, when there was no answer, he went to the nearest window and peered inside the living room, expecting to see Norris asleep in his armchair in front of the television.

The television was on, but Norris wasn't there.

Running out of patience and shivering with cold and anxiety, Albie opened the front door and went inside. He found the downstairs rooms empty. In the kitchen, a cold meal of baked beans on toast was untouched on the dining table next to Norris's reading glasses and a folded newspaper. A mug of tea had been left on the kitchen worktop, and had been cold for a while.

Crumbs on a cutting board and encrusted hobs on the cooker. A dead fly lay upturned by the fruit bowl. The ceiling light buzzed and gave a soft whine. The sink gurgled.

Norris and his wife, who'd been dead for several years, smiled at Albie from an old photo in a silver frame. The house smelled vaguely of boiled sweets in round tins, and beneath that was a taint of damp wood he recognised from log piles left outside under thin tarpaulin in the autumn.

He expected to find Norris dead in his bed upstairs, but there were only empty rooms. He tried to call the police, but each time he pressed dial and put the phone to his ear, the line was filled with a shrill, constant ringing that only stopped when he ended the call. Further attempts to get through failed, and left him frustrated and wincing from the pain in his afflicted eardrum. The ringing echoed inside his head until it slowly faded away. It took several minutes for his hearing to readjust.

He stood at the foot of the stairs and trembled, stifling the panic and harsh sobs building in his throat. One hand was at his face. The house seemed to have more than its fair share of shadows, especially when viewed from the corners of his eyes, and he didn't linger after confirming that Norris was gone.

When he went back outside, into the rain, he glimpsed a figure standing in a downstairs window of the house across the street. The house belonged to Simon and Jane Parish. Albie froze, squinting and wiped his eyes, unsure of what he thought he'd seen. But now it was gone. The figure had been indistinct, backlit by the frail light of a standing lamp in the room behind it, mostly obscured by shadow. Its head had appeared lumpen upon a squat neck, and for a moment Albie thought the figure was wearing several misshapen wigs heaped upon one another.

He was sure that the figure had raised one hand, gesturing for him to come over, and then it had retreated from the window, deeper into the room, fully lost within the shadows inside the house.

I V

CHAPTER FOUR

Claustrophobia hit him as soon as he entered the house across the road. After knocking on the front door without response, he'd gone inside and found himself in a dim hallway with hanging coats, scarves and jackets covering a portion of wall to his left, and a stairway ahead and to the right of him. The gathered coats and scarves smelled of damp in the frigid air and seemed to crowd against him. Between the wall and the stairway, a corridor ran to a starkly-lit kitchen at the back of the house. An unseen clock ticked the seconds away. Nothing moved down there. Halfway along the corridor was the door that led to the living room, where the figure had appeared to him.

He was shivering, clasping his hands to his stomach, on the verge of hysteria and caught in the knowledge that something terrible had happened in Penbrook.

The stink of offal and murder came to him before he'd even opened the living room door. And when he entered that room, hesitant on weak legs, all he could do was stand there with his hands at his face and his eyes stretched wide, staring at the thing in the corner.

It was a totem of some kind, reaching almost to the ceiling, and composed of the broken and mutilated corpses of wild animals and domestic pets. A column of flesh and gristle sewn together from separate parts. Foxes and badgers, dogs and cats, rabbits, deer, pheasants and stoats, all mounted and melded together in twisted designs and accommodating shapes. There were songbirds too, only noticeable by the occasional protrusion of a yellow beak from the amalgamation of entwined flesh and bone. The light from the lamp revealed limbs and ribcages and mammalian snouts. Leaking maws. Feral grimaces and glazed eyes. Tongues spilling from yawning mouths of incisors and black-mottled gums. Splintered bone, tufts of fur and feathers. Trotters amidst dripping hides. Cartilage and shredded muscle. Evisceration.

A tribute of meat and skin.

Discarded animal parts and loose hair lay scattered around the edges of the room. Bodily organs and steaming hearts, glistening flaps of stomach and livers. Slippery membrane. The leftovers of gutted creatures.

Albie hunched over at the hot, awful smells of excrement, kidney and intestines thickening the air, and dry-heaved until his throat was raw. His feet slipped on patches of blood in the carpet. He could taste it all. He wiped his mouth and straightened, his eyes watering as the room shifted around him. The walls reared and fell. He backed up against one side of the doorway, shaking his head against what felt like treacle around his skull, clenching his hands at his sides as he tried to breathe through the tightening of his throat. He made a low sound from his barely open mouth.

The totem, the sculpture of flesh and bone, was an obscene thing in the living room. It shouldn't have existed anywhere, except in the imaginations of the deranged and murderously insane.

'God in heaven,' he managed to whisper. 'Help me. Please help me.'

X

Albie staggered from the living room and leaned against the wall in the corridor outside. He breathed and spat. The images of the horrific flesh sculpture were seared into his mind. He spoke Milly's name and wiped tears from his eyes.

It took him a few moments to become aware of the man standing in the kitchen doorway.

Turning on unsteady, awkward legs, Albie regarded the man and then wished he'd run away instead, because the man's face was terribly loose like an ill-fitting mask pulled over a misshapen skull. He was stripped to the waist, his pallid belly hanging over the waist of his trousers. He stood on bare feet. In his right hand he carried a plastic bag sloshing with raw meat and stolen hearts. His slack mouth was moving silently, forming unheard words, a soundless incantation. His neck leaned slightly to one side, as if his spine was stricken by a grievous injury.

This man was Simon Parish, and Albie had known him, but not like this. Not like this.

Simon Parish smiled to show teeth stained brown and blackened at their ends, behind which a vivid red tongue swayed and squirmed in a grotesque dance.

Albie began to back away, up the corridor towards the front door. The sound of creaking steps brought his attention to the staircase, which Jane was slowly descending with a manic grin, her movements disjointed and jerking, the angles of her body all wrong beneath her dressing gown. Her eyes, deep set within her puffy, bruised face, focused on Albie with gleeful intent.

'Worms live inside me,' she muttered with a swollen mouth. Her teeth were gone.

Albie was at the door when Jane paused to vomit a yolky fluid into her cupped hands. Simon let out a burst of laughter muffled by his gnashing jaws. He pointed at Albie and smiled again, his body twitching and swaying. Jane looked towards Albie with a meek expression of embarrassment then came down the stairs after him as he threw open the door and fled into the rain.

CHAPTER FIVE

Almost witless with terror, Albie ran to his car and dug his hands into his pockets to find his keys, but he couldn't locate them, and he was overcome by panic as he realised he'd dropped them somewhere during his search of the houses.

The rain drenched him. He cried out. And from the far end of the street, where the houses fell away to trees and scrubland, some unseen animal or beast too large to be indigenous responded with a screeching wail that wiped all coherent thought from his mind. It sounded primordial, immense, unknown. Tortured. Slapping his hands over his ears, dizzy from the reverberation of the creature's call, he looked to the end of the street and glimpsed a pale, squalid mass swoop across the road to vanish into the rain and the night. A thing made of wet limbs and flesh bristling with nubs and pustules. The streetlights flickered, and when the beast wailed again Albie forgot about his keys and his car, and staggered away, sobbing and sniffling into his hands.

He fled towards the centre of the village.

Through the sound of falling rain, he heard children singing in the houses.

X

He hurried along as fast as his legs could take him, without a clue where he was going. The inside of his head spun and black grains pulsed upon his vision. His eyes ached, and he thought he was half-mad. Bestial shrieking and grunting all around him, muffled by the rain. A woman's heavy sobbing rose from the drain grate at the roadside. In some windows of the houses he passed, forms of spindly and yellowish flesh writhed and capered. One of the houses was full of strobing lights and inhuman screams. A voice harsh with pain and belligerence called out to him from a darkened bungalow and repeated his name.

Albie halted in the road and screamed, put his hands to his face and pushed at his eyes and then scratched at the soft skin of his cheeks until he was bleeding. He fell to his knees, soaked in puddles, beaten down by the rain. The realisation that he was losing himself was only an absent thought, and then his mind fell away and he lay down on the tarmac in the middle of the road and trembled, muttering the names of obscure gods and celestial things.

The sounds of the village faded, became barely audible.

And just before he passed out, an old woman, drenched to the skin, stood over him and looked down at his pathetic form. She eyed him with the indifference of an apathetic creature. Then she hunched over and grabbed his hands and pulled him from the road.

VI

CHAPTER SIX

There were dreams of visions in which dead cities stood dark under a black sun and glistening entities dwelled in the spaces between the spaces. He saw the faces of men, and one man in particular, who tittered from behind a mask of bronze metal. There was darkness, immeasurable and endless, and old gods sleeping within starless voids and dreaming the dreams of the forgotten.

X

Albie woke on a carpeted floor to the sound of the woman speaking from an adjacent room. Her voice carried through the doorway. Rain slapped at the window. A candle burned on a small table next to him, while another one offered flickering light in the other room. Aside from the candles, the house was dark.

'…all the boys and girls went to play; went to go far away…' Her voice lowered to a whisper, and Albie couldn't make out her following words except for a mention of spidery things in a baby's cradle. She sounded sad and resigned.

Albie stood and wavered, blood rushing too fast through his head. He gritted his teeth against the dull pain in his skull. The living room smelled of dust and lavender. Stacks of yellowed newspapers were piled on the old sofa. An armchair covered in a floral pattern; the wallpaper was of similar design. A painting on the wall, above the cold and soot-streaked fireplace, showed a group of indistinct figures prancing in a dense meadow, their thin arms raised towards a red moon.

He went out to the woman, to a kitchen that hadn't been cleaned in years. Dead insects carpeted the windowsill, where a flower slowly withered, dying of thirst. He had to put his hand over his nose at the pungent reek coming out of the sink filled with sopping rags.

All was silent outside the house. Inside, a clock ticked in a shadowed corner high up the wall.

Her back to Albie and facing the far end of the kitchen, the woman continued to speak, seemingly lost in a stream of consciousness, her voice slowly rising again. She was sitting at the dining table, her hands laid primly and flat in front of her. Grey hair, slick with rainwater, fell past her shoulders. Her woollen cardigan, sodden and tatty, clung to her willowy form. She tapped the little finger of one hand on the table top.

'The people of the village have gone away,' she said, without looking at Albie. 'Mostly everyone. Gone to that other place. But some things come and go as they please. Some things come here. Horrible things. Devils in the night.'

Albie walked around to the other end of the table and looked at her. She stopped talking. The eyes in her gaunt face lifted to regard him, and there was nothing in them but sorrow.

'What happened here?' Albie said. He tried to sound firm and not terrified, but the tremor in his voice betrayed him. 'My wife – I mean, my ex-wife – and my daughter, are gone. Where are they? Do you know where they are?'

'There are survivors at the church,' she said. 'You should probably go to the church. Your family might be there.'

'I have to find them,' he said. 'I can't lose them.'

A tear rolled down the woman's face. 'This is not a Christian place. Not anymore.' And with that she rose from the table, walked to the front door, opened it and disappeared into the rain.

X

After closing the door and locking it with a brass key found nearby, he sat at the dining table, trembling in his clothes, and cried for a long while with his head in his hands. The rain never ceased to fall, and the constant pattering against the kitchen window was maddening.

He thought of Kathleen and Milly. He thought of good times and the bad times afterwards. A deep sense of self-hatred and guilt almost paralysed him. Everything was numb and blurry beyond the pain of loss, grief and unbridled terror.

'I'm sorry,' he muttered. He wiped his eyes and then his mouth. 'I'm sorry that I didn't get to you in time. Where are you? Where have you gone?'

There was no answer except the rain.

A while later, a naked man with arcane symbols cut into his skin stood outside the kitchen window and said that God was a sadist. His forehead was swollen, bulging and pulsing from within, above wicked eyes the colour of jaundice, and he smiled a terrible smile that suggested little sympathy.

Albie screamed for the man to go away, and the man did, but only after he'd reached inside his mouth and down his throat and pulled out a squirming red worm no less than twenty inches long. It was a blind thing, with a lack of sensory organs, but its mouth was all teeth and the man was content to let it suckle at his throat as he walked away into the rain.

VII

CHAPTER SEVEN

He searched for car keys in the house, but when he realised there was nothing on the driveway he gave up and sat on the tattered sofa in the living room, trying to decide his next step.

Something skittered across the roof, claws scrabbling on slate and tiles. His heart quickened as he looked towards the ceiling. He listened and waited, wondering what had come to visit him, and then there was scraping and scratching as the visitor began to slowly descend the chimney. Soot fell and billowed inside the cold fireplace. Albie tracked the pawing and bumping down the wall until it paused near the foot of the chimney space. Black granules and smoky powder tumbled and scattered, speckling the carpet and itching in Albie's throat. It was followed by a burst of low, sly laughter, much like a child's, but different, as if mimicked by an older voice.

And when the voice spoke, breathless and excited, mixed with the damp squirming of something against the brickwork in the confined space, Albie fled the house and didn't look back.

X

Madness waited in the streets and welcomed him as he stumbled through the rain. A man covered in tumours, emaciated and crawling on all fours, reached out to Albie as he passed.

'Have you been saved, brother?'

Farther on, flashes of pale light burst from the windows of houses. Albie glimpsed several people watching him from gardens and flooded yards. They wore white garments and their faces were without skin. They observed him in silence, unbothered by the rain.

An effigy of cloth, straw and sticks in charity shop clothes and propped up on a wooden chair, awaited him in the middle of the road. He thought it was a representation of himself; a cruel joke to taunt him before he was finally taken.

He was still thinking about it when the lights went out in the village and all was darkness.

X

Footfalls behind him, growing louder and then fading, like dwindling echoes. Cold hands brushed against his arms and shoulders, and his whimpers became cries when faces made of writhing tendrils and yawning mouths flashed past him in the light of his phone, which he used as a torch to navigate the dark street.

He screamed when something with a glistening black hide and leathery wings swooped across the road and vanished into the dark. It left a terrible ammonia reek in its wake. Albie doubled over and vomited up the dregs from his stomach.

He carried on, trying to regain his bearings and find the church. The village's topography seemed to have changed since the lights went out – the houses seemed further away from the road and trees stood where he was certain they hadn't before. Their branches were oily black and dripping, and elongated shadows flitted in the upper reaches of their boughs. The air was thick with an off-meat taint, even in the rain.

A loud voice rose from a side road: 'God has abandoned us.'

VIII

CHAPTER EIGHT

He found the church after what seemed like hours of searching, and by then he was exhausted and traumatised, bedraggled and hysteric, soaked to the skin and on his knees. The village had shown him all its new delights and infrequent guests. Immense monsters formed of black flesh and squirming appendages had been glimpsed beyond the gaps between houses, and their great onyx limbs had risen above the roofs and the squat buildings and reached towards the falling sky before being obscured by the rain.

He banged both hands on the heavy front doors of the church, vaguely aware of the thin shapes moving languidly behind him, and he listened to them chatter and laugh and talk of the God of Gods. And when the church doors opened, the creatures scurried away, still laughing and splashing through puddles. Albie thought they might have been children once.

The man in the doorway looked down at Albie and said nothing. Sullen eyes within a face roughened by a heavy beard. Wide shoulders inside a trench coat.

Albie whimpered, raising his face to the man in the church. 'I was told to come here.'

The man seized Albie with large, powerful hands and hauled him out of the rain. The doors slammed shut and a bolt was thrown. Lying on the stone floor, breathless and shaking, Albie glimpsed the high roof of the church and candlelight all around him, and then he closed his eyes and darkness seeped into his mind to give him respite from the terrors of the village.

X

A dream followed, in which a chorus of tortured voices bayed and wailed from abyssal depths. Sheer agony in the cries of the lost ones within the void. Their pain was beyond comprehension.

In those black depths between worlds, they were hunted by gods and abominations.

X

The reverend was standing over him when he woke on the floor of the old church, dripping wet and gasping. The man's narrow eyes regarded him, and his mouth was a vague, stoic line within the tangled beard. He was well over six feet tall.

'I thought you were a mad fellow,' the reverend said.

Albie rose onto his elbows, wincing at the shuddering pain in his legs. He felt weighed down, burdened with shame and guilt, his mind brimming with images of the things that had come to him in the dark.

'Thank you for letting me in,' he said, coughing to clear his throat. He wiped his wet face.

The reverend shrugged. 'Looks like you took a black pilgrimage to this place.'

'What?'

The big man helped him to his feet and said no more.

Albie brushed water from his clothes and looked at the man. 'It's me, Reverend Cottam. Albie Samways. You know me.'

Cottam's face was without expression, and no words of acknowledgement were offered. He smelled of damp cowhide and muddy boots. A lone muscle twitched under his left eye. One corner of his mouth trembled. Albie wondered what he had seen that night.

'Don't you recognise me?' Albie said. 'I've known you for years. I've been here before…'

'They let you live,' said Cottam, his voice plain and without inflection. 'Must be a reason for that.'

A monster shrieked out in the dark, and Albie swivelled his head towards the front doors of the church.

Cottam sniffed, wiped his damp nose. 'They haven't tried to get in. Yet.' He turned his back on Albie and walked up the aisle. Albie took in his surroundings, looking for threats from the darkened corners and lightless spaces in the upper reaches of the arched ceilings. The church was full of shadows. Wind whistled and sighed in the old walls. No lull in the rain.

Albie's breath spilled in plumes in the cold air. He was shivering in his wet clothes, his arms folded as he shifted on his feet. He felt hopeless.

Out of sight, from somewhere within the shadows of the chancel, Cottam called to him.

'Do you want a drink, friend?'

IX

CHAPTER NINE

They sat in the pews, passing the whiskey bottle back and forth. The alcohol put soothing warmth in Albie's stomach and subdued the shaking of his hands.

'What happened here?' he asked the reverend.

Cottam exhaled through his mouth and gave a pained expression. He stared at the floor between his feet, head lowered so that Albie couldn't see his eyes. He took a long swig of whiskey and held the bottle to his chest. When he spoke, his voice was little more than a whisper.

'It started just after the sun went down and the rain began. In the dusk deepening to night and darkness was when they emerged. You wouldn't believe it, friend. I saw one of the entities, and it saw me, so I ran before it could catch me. I tried to stop them by pleading to God, but it was already too late for the village and the people here. It's too late for all of us.'

'What are they?' Albie said.

'You've seen them. They've reached out and touched you. They have tolerated you, friend.'

Albie tightened one hand into a fist and held it in his lap. 'My ex-wife and daughter are gone. Where have they gone?'

A grimace passed over the reverend's face. 'They were taken.'

'Taken where?'

'A place beyond this place.'

'What?'

'A place beyond this world, friend.'

Albie shook his head and pinched between his eyes as the world wavered around him. He bit back on the hysteria juddering in his throat. 'This is madness. This is fucking madness.'

Cottam regarded him with a knowing look. 'You've seen them. You've seen the things. You've been in their presence.'

Albie said nothing, lost for words and rational thoughts. He took the whiskey from the reverend's hand and took a long pull on the bottle. When he was finished he was gasping and nauseated. He wanted to cry.

'Abandon hope,' the reverend whispered. 'God is dead.'

Tears welled in Albie's eyes. 'Do you remember me at all? Your name is Marcus Cottam. You've been the vicar of this church for over fifteen years. You christened my daughter. Don't you remember?'

'None of that matters anymore,' Cottam said.

'I refuse to believe that. There has to be a way to get my family back.'

The reverend took back the bottle and swigged. Wiped his mouth with the back of one hand. 'People were drawn into the dark, the spaces between the spaces, and now they're lost. Lost in Hell, I think. And some of the devils from Hell came here, and they're having a whale of time. The beasts of the wastelands. Entities that shouldn't exist. Unspeakable things. Nameless forms.'

'Are you saying there's nothing I can do to bring them back?'

The muscles that formed the shape of Cottam's face twitched and trembled. His mouth was agape as he stared at the ceiling, as if he was silently beseeching the god he no longer seemed to believe in. Then he looked at Albie and there was something like a sad smile, with resignation and heartbreak in his eyes. And he pulled a serrated kitchen knife from inside his coat and held it in a shaking hand whose palms were calloused and raw.

Albie didn't move.

Cottam said, 'I'm glad you came here. It was nice to share a final drink with someone still human. I couldn't have done this, otherwise. I couldn't have done this on my own.'

Albie was too slow to stop him.

'Christ, receive my soul,' Cottam muttered, and before Albie could reach him, he laid his head back to expose his throat and began slashing through skin, muscle, and meat, spluttering and gasping at the ceiling, before the blade went deep and found an artery.

Albie stumbled away and fell down in the aisle. Cottam gurgled and choked, slumping and convulsing as blood gushed and spilled from the ruin of his throat. Arterial spray doused the pew and the floor below. His hands dropped into his lap and the knife clattered away from him. He uttered a strangled cry from between clenched teeth, which was followed by the sound of sopping wetness and fluid splatter, and then his mouth yawned open and he retched and twitched until the flow of blood faltered and slowly dripped and dwindled to nothing as his heart stopped. He fell quiet after a final, croaking sigh and slumped forward on the back of the pew in front.

Albie scrambled to his feet, touching the flecks of Cottam's blood on his face. He could taste the hot reek of iron in the air. 'Oh God, oh God...' He bit down on the knuckles of one hand and backed against a stone pillar, staring at the dead man, near-witless and gawping. His mind was breaking. He was losing himself, losing reality, weak-limbed and numb with terror. Dark patches bloomed upon his vision then vanished. His chest hitched with each breath and his entire body shuddered. It felt like everything inside him was falling away.

He was only vaguely aware of the change in air pressure and the sense of movement behind him. He turned and saw a tall, thin figure in a bronze mask and a gown of dull white cloth standing at the end of the aisle. Deep shadows, deeper than they had been before, obscured the back of the church behind the spindly figure. Lengths and tufts of long, wispy, nicotine-yellow hair flowed from the top and both sides of the figure's mask. The hair of someone old and sickly. Wet eyes, pinkish and inflamed, centred upon Albie from within the holes in the mask. The mouth hole was a narrow rectangular slit through which scabbed lips parted to reveal an abundance of gritted teeth. Like a pained smile within a skull. The figure's hands were empty and shockingly pale. It appeared to be a man, but Albie couldn't be sure. His bones ached, corrupted with cold and fatigue, his strength was slipping away, and the breaking of his heart left him resigned to the fate that awaited him, most likely to be dealt by the masked visitor and its friends in the shadows.

And those friends emerged from the dark behind the figure, slowly defining with indistinct angles and edges in the candlelight. Some were burdened with twisted limbs and palsied hands, disjointed and deformed. Some of them appeared barely human, with flayed faces and bulbous eyes. People of the village, a few of them dressed in pale gowns similar to the masked figure.

Several dozen of the villagers came forward and gathered around the masked one. Albie looked for Kathleen and Milly amongst them, but he didn't see their faces, and the absolute lack of hope was enough that he would have taken Cottam's knife for his own use if he could have moved. Tears ran down his face and heavy sobs became stuck like knots in his throat. He glimpsed engorged figures and terribly thin apparitions amongst the villagers. Flailing shadows capered all around, and Albie caught a brief sighting of something with dripping tendrils and bloated flesh sacs clambering across the ceiling high above. A braying shriek rose from the street beyond the churchyard. Some terrible thing responded with a similar call.

When he turned back to the aisle, the masked man was standing before him, no more than two yards away. The figure smelled of spoiled pork, and its bloodshot eyes appraised him. The mouth curled a little at one side.

'What did you do?' said Albie. 'What did you do to this place?'

The figure took hold of Albie's shoulders and guided him down to the floor. The shadow-haunted flock of villagers watched, and some whispered to each other with hands covering their faces. On his knees, Albie sobbed, muttering his daughter's name, waiting for death or madness.

The masked apparition said nothing. The only sound was a slight wheezing from behind the mask.

Albie would have begged for mercy if he had the breath in his lungs, but all he could was silently scream as the man forced his hands inside his mind and took an obscene act of communion inside this holy place.

PART TWO

X

CHAPTER TEN

Albie woke muddled in sweat-dampened sheets and blankets and grasped for the glass of water on the bedside table. Fragments of troubled dreams remained half-remembered, with glimpses of faces and languid forms, scenes from barren rooms and the screaming mouths of tortured men. He sat up, wincing from aches and cramps in his tired muscles and dry joints. He drank from the glass, relieving his throat with the dusty water, and when he was done he slumped against the headboard and wiped his mouth then blinked at the dim daylight that filled the window beyond the foot of his bed. There was the faint barking of a dog somewhere in the neighbourhood, the low growl of car exhausts mixed with jumbled voices raised in anger or excitement, and below it all was the dampened thrum of the town like a black heart awakening in the start of another day.

He sagged like a wretched thing amongst the wrappings of his bed. Sometimes when he woke it was hard to remember where he lived, and even more difficult to recall anything specific from the last five years since that night in the village of Penbrook.

He rose, pulled on his jeans and his old Iron Maiden t-shirt then swallowed his various pills and medications. In the cold room, he stood shivering and hungry, listening to the sounds of the building around him. The old walls, the cracked plaster in the ceiling, the aged angles and corners stained with damp. The tenant in the neighbouring room was laughing.

Albie checked the time, and with the late hour of the morning he was relieved not to have work today. There hadn't been any work for the last two weeks. He put on his jacket and trainers and left his room, locking the door behind him. He stepped out onto the windowless landing and wrinkled his nose at the low smell of soiled clothes left in bins. A grey light rose from the hallway down the stairs on the ground floor. A bare lightbulb painted the walls in jaundice. The doors to the other tenants' rooms remained mercifully closed. He had no patience for their anxieties and musty scents this morning.

In the room directly across from him someone muttered in a foreign language from behind the door. It sounded Slavic. In another room a television played too loud, trembling in the walls, mixed with the clank and cluttering of dishes in a metal sink. Someone groaned from beyond a throat of stairs rising to the second and top floor.

Albie hurried across the landing to the communal bathroom and tried the door, and when it opened he peered inside and found it empty, locked the door behind him, relieved and sickened and already tired in his bones. The bathroom smelled of the encrusted pipes feeding from the toilet. Grey patches of damp clouded the ceiling. The soles of his trainers stuck to the grimy tiled floor, where stains of unknown provenance surrounded him.

The yellowed toilet seat was damp, so he wiped it dry with the last of the tissue pulled from the cardboard roll. There was piss in the unflushed toilet bowl. He added his own and flushed, then washed his hands and splashed his face and ran his fingers through his scraggly beard. He placed his hands on the sink, leaned forward with his head lowered and tried not to look at his reflection.

CHAPTER ELEVEN

Albie was out of the bedsit thirty minutes later. It was almost midday. He walked the streets for an hour, aimless and meandering, and scraped together enough money from his pockets to buy a coffee and a bacon sandwich from a dilapidated café with grimy windows and sullen serving staff. He sat at a table in one corner, avoiding eye contact with the other customers. Men in work gear and old boots frowned over red-top tabloids and drank greased tea. The smell of pork fat permeated everything. His coffee tasted of chemicals, but he drank it, glad for the warmth inside him. He kept the uneaten crusts from his sandwich and put them in one pocket of his coat.

When he stepped outside he noticed a spindly, blackened figure with a sagging pot belly and excited, glaring eyes crouching in the shadowed mouth of an alleyway across the street, but he turned away before he saw its face. And when he looked again a few moments later the figure was gone and the echo of its plaintive voice was most likely the wind sweeping through the grey street.

X

He went to the local park and fed crusts from his sandwich to the ducks on the river. There were no walkers on the paths, or parents and children in the playground. A seagull wheeled overhead, its piercing staccato shrieks slowly fading as it flapped away.

As he tossed the scraps of bread to the water and the squabbling birds, he looked about for lone figures that might be watching him. His shoulders tensed and parts of him trembled. He watched for odd shapes and tall things loping between the trees, but there was nothing and he was glad of that.

He remembered the blackened figure in the alleyway, and a cold shade passed through his blood. Beads of sweat broke through the skin of his face and he bit his lip to stifle a low whimper. He shivered. Then he took and held a deep breath before releasing it from his chest with a shudder. His rattling heart slowed and found its level.

'Christ. Christ almighty.'

He'd grown accustomed to the sightings, the visitations and the awful sounds he sometimes heard below the noise of the world. The manifestations of terrible forms and effigies, the capering apparitions, the lurking shadows of monsters, all of them like horrific remnants and reminders of what he'd experienced in Penbrook. Avatars and arbiters, messengers and heralds. Hints and clues revealed in his dreams and nightmares. They had taken the villagers, spirited them away – that much he knew – but there was little else, apart from the certainty that Kathleen and Milly were dead and gone.

The first specks of drizzle fell against his face, and he turned away from the river and the feeding birds and made for the dense streets of human life.

X

The church stood squat and weathered at one corner of a four-way intersection on the western edge of the town. The headlights of cars and trucks swept and glared in the downpour as Albie hurried along the pavement and through the large, open doors of the church. He stood in the vestibule and looked around, rainwater dripping from his shoulders. The pews were empty of the faithful. Before he started up the aisle, he glanced back at the doorway to check he hadn't been followed, and scolded himself for his latent paranoia.

He sat down at the edge of a pew near the front and rubbed his hands together for warmth, unsure why he'd come here for shelter. After seeing such sights in Penbrook, any vague notion of a benevolent God seemed like a cruel joke to him. But he lowered his head because it always felt like the right thing to do after sitting down in a church.

He shook his head and bit down on a burst of laughter that came from the red chambers inside his mind.

'Hello, Albie.'

He raised his head as Reverend Blythe appeared in the aisle beside him. He hadn't even heard her approach. Wiping his face, he looked up at her and offered a faint smile that barely curled his mouth.

'Hello, Reverend.'

'You all right, Albie?'

He nodded quicker than he should have. 'Just wanted to get out of the rain for a while.'

Blythe sat down on the pew in front of Albie's and half-turned to regard him. She had a kind face. Her grey hair was tied into a neat bun, and combined with her spectacles gave her a bookish appearance that put Albie at ease.

'It's a bit nasty out there,' she said.

'I don't like the rain.'

'How have you been?'

Albie looked at her, then away. 'I've been fine.'

'Keeping busy?'

'Trying to.'

'That's good.'

'I hope so.'

'Would you like a cup of tea?'

'No thanks,' he replied.

'Has something happened?'

Albie found himself looking at her again, but he said nothing. He wiped his mouth, glanced to his sides then regarded her with watery eyes that blurred his vision before he wiped them clear. He swallowed an unpleasant taste in his throat. 'Nothing's happened.'

'Okay,' said Blythe.

'You don't believe me?'

'I didn't say that.'

Albie's eyes drifted to his lap. His hands were clasped together upon his thighs and his knuckles were bloodless. Dirt darkened his fingernails.

'What's wrong, Albie?' Blythe said. 'You come in here twice a week, looking like you're being chased by someone. If something's wrong, you can tell me. I can help you.'

'I don't think you can help me.'

'You'd be surprised. I'd meant to ask you before, but do you believe, at all?'

'Not really.'

'That's okay. I can still help you.'

His smile towards her was pathetic, trembling at the corners. 'If I told you my problems, you wouldn't believe me.'

'Try me.'

'It's best you don't know. You don't want to see the things I've seen.'

'What have you seen?'

'I can't tell you.'

'What happened to you, Albie?'

He let out a ragged breath and sagged upon the bench. He could smell his damp clothes and the musty reek of stale sweat beneath them. Close to tears, he screwed his eyes shut and clenched his hands into fists, and he was about to confess all to Blythe when the rain outside stopped and the only sound was the crashing of his pulse in his ears. He rose from the pew, thanked Blythe for her time, and staggered back down the aisle with the reverend's voice following him through the doorway and calling for him to come back.

He hurried back to the squalor of the bedsit and his pathetic room.

XII

CHAPTER TWELVE

Darkness fell with more rain and an emptying of the streets, and Albie sat locked in his room, slumping on his bed with his photo album on his lap and a bottle of vodka beside him. He leafed through the pages and looked at the photos of Kathleen and Milly taken over the years.

He drank the vodka straight from the bottle and savoured the numbing of his insides from each mouthful. He sobbed into his hands and he said the names of his family; he called to them, pleaded to them, begged for their return, but nothing was to be done and there was nothing he could do. But he did this each night, a ritual of sorts, until he drank enough and passed out.

Tonight it took most of a bottle to put him under.

And then he was gone, gone to dream, travelling to places where the dead waited for him.

X

He'd been found witless and catatonic, wandering the fallow fields just outside Penbrook on the morning after the disappearance of over two thousand villagers. Covered in mud and drenched with rainwater, muttering with his hands at his mouth, his clothes torn and ragged. A bedraggled thing with no sense of self or place, shouting the names of old gods at the police officers as they went to help him. And then there were paramedics, a stretcher of some sort, and the inside of an ambulance with plastic things and wires attached to him. He'd cried and wailed, raved about monsters on thin legs and the figure in the bronze mask. He'd told them about the rain and the abominations, but the paramedics merely soothed and sedated him. They made no acknowledgement of his manic confessions.

Then the men from the government arrived, and that was that.

X

Albie snapped awake sometime during the night and heard the man in the next room lament about lost things and cry against the other side of the wall. Then the man fell silent, with just the slapping and scraping of his hands upon bare plaster, and Albie went back to sleep.

X

Once he'd physically recovered from his ordeal in Penbrook, the men from the government took Albie to a hidden place of dour buildings and fences. They repeated questions to him in sterile rooms, while observers watched and took notes from behind one-way mirrors.

He had few answers for them and no explanation except for the speculation of his damaged mind. They ran tests on his brain, bones and soft organs, took blood and rushed it away in vials and tubes. He endured x-rays and intimate scans that sapped his energy. They forced him to sign non-disclosure agreements and hinted at what would happen to him if he shared his experiences with the outside world. They sectioned him for his own safety, placing him in an institute for the mad and the lost. He spent twenty-eight months there, until his mind healed from the trauma and he regained his senses and made no more attempts on his own life.

Upon his release, with everything lost, he moved to the north of England and worked odd jobs between bouts of unemployment. Christmases and the birthdays of his lost loved ones were bad times for him. He soothed his troubles with medication and alcohol. Painkillers took the edge from things. He became a transient amongst the dregs of society, and forgot the best parts of himself.

But he never forgot his family and never would.

XIII

CHAPTER THIRTEEN

The morning arrived in grey and fog and cold. He put away the photo album and the mementoes of his past life, along with the takeaway cartons and the empty vodka bottle. He dressed quickly, and was out of the bedsit soon afterwards, cowed and hunched, hurrying along the pavement and making sure not to look at the writhing forms in his peripheral vision.

Something tall and shockingly thin in tattered clothes flitted behind him, and swept across the road and away before vanishing.

He returned to the park and stood at the side of the river as the ducks swam towards him. The park was busier today, with joggers weaving between dog walkers, tired-looking mothers pushing prams, and old married couples holding hands as they strolled. A man and his son flew a kite, watching it flap and swerve within eddies and gusts high above them. Somewhere nearby a baby cried. Crows and magpies loitered in the trees at the boundaries of the park.

The expectant ducks drifted away from the river's edge when he showed them his empty hands. He flinched whenever he thought a speck of rain landed on his skin. Beyond the human din, he thought he heard distant voices and cries that could only come from the malformed mouths of beasts.

He closed his eyes and considered his future, trying to decide if it was worth the pain of loneliness and squalor. He saw himself as an old man, a wretched specimen beyond salvation or relief, with the only chance of an escape inside vodka bottles and packets of pills. He saw himself dying in poverty, fading from the map, forgotten in ash and bone.

A little voice said his name, as though the speaker was standing next to him. He opened his eyes and looked about, but no one stood with him, and he thought it must have been his mind. He had almost convinced himself, when he glanced over at a cluster of oak trees beyond the river on the far side of the park.

Milly stood in the shadows under the heavy boughs, looking towards him. She wore a makeshift dress of dull white rags that reached to her ankles and left her arms bare. She hadn't aged in five years.

Albie caught a glimpse of her face, and a brief smile that seemed pained and hopeful. His mouth fell open and he held out one hand for something to hold him upright, but he only grasped at thin air and slipped on the wet grass and fell to one knee, his heart faltering. He sucked in a breath and climbed to his feet, not taking his eyes from the trees.

Milly seemed to step back – or was *pulled* – into the shadows, and it was as if she'd never been there at all. And only shadows remained where she'd been standing.

Albie staggered over the wooden bridge that spanned the river and hurried to the oak trees as he muttered Milly's name and begged for her to return. But there was no sign of her in the weeds, reeking mulch, and drifts of rotting acorns. No shoeprints except for his own. Frantic and breathless, he searched for his daughter in the vicinity, raising his voice so that people in the park gave him curious or concerned looks as they walked past. A little boy pointed and laughed, before his parents pulled him away from the strange man.

Soon he was alone, and he put his hands over his face to sob and curse. And he cowered as the screams of monstrous things no one else could hear echoed in the sky.

'Help me,' he said to no one. 'Please help me.'

He fled from the park, shades whispering on his heels.

X

Back in his room, he locked the door and sat with his back against it and closed his eyes to the sounds of hands slapping against the walls on the landing. Placing his hands over his ears, he gritted his teeth, grinding them until one molar cracked and a sharp pain ignited in his lower jaw. He wondered if his medication was failing, his descent into mania inevitable. The inside of his head spun with a slow madness. He said the names of his family over and over and only stopped when he heard footfalls on the landing. He held his breath, moved one side of his head close to the door.

The footfalls halted outside his room.

He hesitated, rising to his feet, listening, but there was just the distant bawling of an infant in a room near the top of the building, barely heard through the walls and floors.

'Hello?' he said, regretting it immediately, and thought of shuddering, white-eyed creatures that dwelled in shadowed places. He recalled nightmares of carnivorous mouths and needling appendages.

There was no answer.

Against all his instincts of self-preservation, he opened the door, his heart close to failing, but no one awaited him and the landing was empty. He wondered if one of the other tenants had knocked on his door and then quickly slipped back to their room. He didn't like pranks. He didn't like jokers.

He looked down.

Milly's toy bear, the one she had loved since she was a little girl, lay on the tattered carpet of the landing just outside his doorway.

XIV

CHAPTER FOURTEEN

Albie sat on the edge of his bed, staring at the toy bear in his hands. One of its button-eyes was missing. It was a ragtag thing, drowned, pathetic and reeking of decomposing leaves and drains, but when he raised it to his face all he could smell was Milly's dark hair. The bear had been made especially for Milly by Albie's mother shortly before the girl was born. A friend to welcome her into the world.

Albie's mother had died when Milly was two. It was one of his greatest regrets that Milly would never remember her brief time with her grandmother.

He cried for them both, and his lost wife, and waited for the footfalls to return to his door. But they never did, not in all the hours of that day and night.

X

He fell asleep atop the sheets on his bed, and woke up shivering in his clothes, confused and groggy in the darkness of his room. The bear was still in his hands, clutched to his chest like a talisman to ward off bad spirits. The only light came from the streetlamp a few yards down from the lone window in his room.

Blurry fragments of his dream returned to him and made him feel sick with swaying in his gut. Bad feelings and hurt, pain and desperation. Writhing limbs and loping shapes with gleeful faces. He tried to forget them all. He tried to sleep again. But he didn't want to dream. He was sick of dreams.

X

It was another grey morning below a dirty sky. After waking from his restless sleep, Albie stood in the doorway of his room wearing the same clothes he'd worn the day before, and looked out at the landing, as if waiting for the bringer of Milly's bear to return.

Was it someone who'd survived that night in the village? Someone he didn't know about? Was it Milly or Kathleen? He had no idea, and when he tried to think about it his mind became muddled and busy with panicked thoughts, and palpitations seized his heart. His stomach broiled and reared with a queasy feeling he couldn't shake.

He returned to the park, trembling with apprehension and something like hope. Creeping dread filled the back of his mind. He spat onto the grass, wiped his mouth, moved along the path through the park, crossed the bridge over the river, and stood by the oak trees where he'd seen Milly. Beyond the tall oaks, a thicket of birches, elms and scraggly vegetation marked the border between the park, and past that was a large expanse of wasteland and a murky council estate. There was little demand for gentrification in the town.

Albie looked around, while keeping one eye on the shadows that seemed to grow from the trees like malignant forms on an x-ray. He held Milly's bear in one hand, gripping it fiercely like a charm. The wind whistled lowly, barely heard, stirring the boughs and pulling at thin branches so that they appeared to reach for him.

He waited all morning and two hours into the afternoon, ignoring the suspicious looks and glances from other people in the park. When he realised he was lurking in a park with a teddy bear in his hand, he worried that someone would call the police. He expected confrontation and questions from concerned individuals, but the people who saw him were either too disinterested or scared to approach. And he didn't blame them, because he looked like a murderous tramp clutching a trophy taken from his last victim.

Albie was about to give up and return to the bedsit when, due to some half-buried instinct, he turned and stared towards the thicket within the oaks.

She was there, waiting for him, a vision in her bedraggled dress and filthy shoes, indistinct within the edge of the thicket, like something grown from within the dark vegetation. Albie's fingers tensed around the bear. His pulse beat madly in his throat. The rest of the world went away and there was only his daughter in the dim light of the grey day.

Milly's eyes met his, then she looked down at the ground, and her face seemed to be frozen with dumb shock. One bare arm swayed at her side, bristling in the leaves of low branches. A sense of great sadness and grief rose from her.

She was an apparition, frail and far away.

XV

CHAPTER FIFTEEN

After she vanished into the thicket, Albie followed and called her name. The light was already starting to fade as he entered the idle ranks of trees and hanging thorns.

He glanced at his surroundings with watery eyes, and there was no sign of her, but he thought he could hear her voice, distant and faint, coming from every direction. He pushed through the scrub and drooping branches, scratched by brambles and stinging nettles. He cried out when something sharp and needle-thin scored a shallow line across his brow. Then, after more pawing and struggling through the trees, he found himself in a bowl-shaped clearing no bigger than his room at the bedsit. The trees crowded the edges, rearing higher than he could stand, with shadows deepening beyond him. The ground was mushy under his trainers. There was the smell of rotting vegetation and wet bark, a fungal stink and the odour of ripe toadstools.

Sniffling and hunched over, he took breaths of air that were thick and grainy with particles he could taste on his tongue. He wiped blood from the scratch on his forehead.

His heart almost stopped when the tall woman in the pale gown emerged from between the trees and stepped into the clearing. A mad thought occurred that she was Kathleen, but then the woman raised her face to him, and all he could do was back away and cry out, almost dropping the teddy bear when he tripped and stumbled on a jutting tree root.

Her face was a mask of skin stretched across a snapping skull, her filth-clotted mouth damp and glistening as she salivated and rasped. Her dark hair reached to her squirming shoulders. And then, with the movement of a shuddering puppet, she jerked forward, arms flailing at the sides of her filthy gown, and fell to her hands and knees and went after him, gibbering like a mad ape.

Albie staggered from the clearing and crashed through the crowding trees and vegetation, losing his sense of direction in the darkened rows and poor light. Behind him the woman squealed and slapped her hands upon the ground. Branches swatted at his face, pushing into his mouth with sour leaves and ridges of bark, and he spluttered and coughed, glancing back every few yards. The edge of the thicket couldn't have been far, but minutes later he was still moving, seeking the end of the trees. And by the time the laces of his trainers snagged on twisting limbs of brambles on the ground and he fell facedown onto muddy grass, his lungs were flat and without air, and his vision quivered with his crashing heartbeat.

He turned onto his back as the woman skittered out of the brush and fell upon him. He screamed with his hands held out to ward her off, as she squealed through her awful mouth. He grabbed her by the arms while she flailed. Her jaws snapped closer to his face. She stank of putrescence and maggot nests. Her palsied hands wandered to his navel and gripped the soft flesh of his stomach. Her nails pierced his skin.

'You,' she rasped, as if it meant anything. She leaned in to draw him into her mouth, her tongue whipping from side-to-side within the gap made by her blackened lips. Her eyes rolled backwards in anticipation, ecstatic and hysterical. She gave a muffled laugh.

With all his strength, still holding the teddy bear, Albie lifted her away and pushed her violently to the ground, where she fell writhing and kicking. He rolled to one side a second before she struck the ground with her dripping hands where he'd lain. He climbed to his feet and fell against the nearest tree, glancing back at the woman as she rose in awkward, gangly movements.

He ran, tearing through the undergrowth and dense foliage, knowing that the woman was right on his heels, scampering on hands and feet like some demented animal.

She was one of the lost villagers of Penbrook and she couldn't have been real, but the smell of her scent upon him and the fingernail wounds in his stomach couldn't be ignored.

He screamed with all the air he had left. He faltered and slowed, despite kicking hard through the brush and hindering vines. His legs gave out and he collapsed. And as he raised his face from the mulch and dirt, the trees seemed to part to allow a shape passage between them, out of the shadows like an ashen ghost.

'Milly,' he whispered.

The girl walked to him. Stood over him, swaying slightly. She looked in the direction he'd come from. She spoke, and her voice almost broke Albie's heart.

'The woman is one of the in-between things, caught between the spaces. She's gone now.'

'Is it really you?' he whispered. He tasted dead leaves in his mouth.

Milly looked down at his prone, disbelieving form. She had indeed aged hardly at all in those five years. 'Some of the villagers suffered that fate; some can cross over from the other places.'

'What places?' Albie asked.

The girl shook her head. 'Terrible places, Dad, full of monsters. Can we go home?'

CHAPTER SIXTEEN

Night had fallen by the time they left the thicket, and the only lights were in the streets beyond the park. Albie placed his coat over Milly's shoulders to keep her warm against the cold and dark of the world, and put one arm around her to keep her close. She radiated cold through her meagre clothes and clung to the bear that Albie had returned to her.

She didn't speak. Her teeth chattered. Exhaustion and trauma silenced her.

Albie suppressed a smile and a surge of hope as he guided her. The thought that this girl was a replica of Milly, a mimic, a cuckoo looking for a warm nest, was pushed to the back of his mind. A sob of relief and elation filled his throat as he looked down at her, because she was his kin, his blood, his beautiful thing, and he would never lose her again.

X

They reached the bedsit without incident. Albie had smuggled Milly into his room and away from the shadows that seemed to follow them in the streets. Now Milly slept in her father's bed, while he watched over her from a wooden chair and drank vodka in the meagre light of a lamp in the corner.

Upon arrival in the room Milly had downed several glasses of tap water and scoffed two packets of crisps without a break between them. She had been ravenous, almost feral in her feeding, and it unsettled Albie a little to watch her tear into her food like some manic thing dragged in from the streets.

After the water and the food, she gave in to exhaustion and passed out on the bed. She was such a thin girl, clutching her raggedy bear to herself. Her eyelids fluttered as she slept and she murmured wordless sounds. Once she cried out, and it was all Albie could do not to leap from his seat and comfort her as if she were an infant. He restrained himself, tears brimming in his eyes, and all he did was reach out and touch her foot to make sure she was real and not some concoction of his frayed mind. Shame burned inside him when he realised how pathetic his life must seem, in his wretched room inside the dismal bedsit.

He was unable to comprehend the past few hours, shocked into a form of passive observance and impotent to do anything more than let his daughter sleep after her five year disappearance. He wondered about her health, as she'd been gone for so long. And where had she gone? Why hadn't she aged? There would be difficult questions in the near future, starting tomorrow. How would her disappearance be explained to the authorities? Would the government want to take her away? What about Kathleen? *Where* was Kathleen?

That last question, he dreaded the most.

He put it all to the back of his mind and listened to Milly's slow breathing in the night. He hoped she was dreaming of good things.

X

Albie was awake as dawn broke over the town. He rose from the chair, wincing at the stiffness in his back, and put one hand to the lowest part of his spine. He stretched and tried to remember his dreams from last night, but only recalled vague images of people with skinless faces muttering into their hands and crying.

Milly woke soon afterwards. She smiled at her father and hugged him as he prepared a breakfast of cereal and toast. He put his arms around her and said he loved her and everything would be all right. They stayed like that for a long while, long after the toast had popped all burnt and blackened.

They ate cereal, sitting together on the edge of his bed. He couldn't stop smiling at her. His heart swelled.

When Milly had finished her food, she looked up at her father, concern in her face.

'Is something wrong?' Albie asked her, dreading the answer.

She placed the empty bowl beside her. 'We have to leave, Dad. Doctor Ridings and his people will find us. They want me to come back to them.'

CHAPTER SEVENTEEN

'What happened to you?' Albie asked her. 'What happened to your mother?' He sat on the wooden chair and faced Milly on the edge of the bed.

The girl held the bear to her stomach, rocking as she stared at the dour carpet. 'We were taken to another place, somewhere beyond this world, where there was suffering and pain. I can't remember much, and not much of it makes sense.' She looked at Albie. 'Mum's dead, Dad.'

He exhaled slowly, biting down on his lower lip. 'How did she die?'

'Something in the spaces between the spaces took her. A monster. A Haunter of the Dark. One of many. People never stopped screaming.'

Albie bunched his hands into fists, the tendons in his wrists and forearms pressing upwards against his skin. He breathed raggedly through his nose and held back tears that were already pooling in his tired eyes.

'It's okay,' he said, biting down on a whimper of grief and watery nausea at the back of his throat. 'You're safe now, Milly, that's all that matters.'

'I'm not safe, Dad. *We're* not safe. Ridings and his followers will come after me.'

'Why?'

'No one is allowed mercy.'

'What does that mean?'

'We have to leave this place, Dad. Please. You have to listen to me.'

'Who is Ridings?'

'Doctor Ridings. He wears a bronze mask. He started it all. He was responsible for what happened in the village.'

Albie remembered the man in the bronze mask standing over him in the church. He remembered screaming as the man ransacked his mind. It was his last memory of that night. He looked at his daughter, but said nothing, gently coaxing her with patience and silence to continue.

'Ridings is the leader of the Flayed.'

'Who are the Flayed?'

'His acolytes. Former people of the village. They were skinned alive, but they didn't die. Ridings wouldn't let them die. He loves them, and they love him. They serve him.'

'I think I've seen them before,' Albie muttered.

'They've been waiting for the chance to return to this world, so they can change it and make it pure, let chaos and gods rule. Monsters can cross over too. Worms live inside some of the people.'

'It's insanity,' Albie said.

'Yes, it is. But it's true. You've seen it all happen, Dad. You saw it in the village.'

'Why does Ridings want you?'

'I can't remember.'

'You can't remember at all?'

'If I did know, I'd tell you.'

'I know.'

'I missed you, Dad.'

He smiled a pained smile. 'I missed you too, rascal.'

They looked at each other for a moment.

'It's really me,' she said. 'I'm not trying to trick you, Dad.'

'I know,' he said, after a second of hesitation. 'But why haven't you aged in five years?'

'I think time moves much slower in some of the other places. It's like only a few months have passed for me. Most of it's like a half-forgotten dream. All these worlds, dimensions, thin places mixed together.'

'The spaces between the spaces,' said Albie.

She nodded. 'The spaces between the spaces.' Then she began crying.

Albie took her in his arms and embraced her. She buried her head against his chest. They cried together.

'Was it you who left your bear here?' he asked.

Her voice was muffled. 'Yes, I did. To let you know it was me. I didn't have time to stop.'

'Okay.'

'Okay, Dad.'

And when Albie noticed rain speckling against the window, he made sure not to let go of his girl, his light against the dark, his little hero.

X

He took her to the communal bathroom and gave her a fresh towel and stood outside the door while she showered. No one came out of the other rooms. He heard the toilet flush.

When she emerged almost half an hour later, the smears of dirt and filth were had been scrubbed from her skin and she looked more human than she did before. Her hair was clean and hung in ropey strands that hadn't yet dried properly. Her crude dress of white cotton rags appeared even more scraggly and pathetic than before.

'We need to find you some new clothes,' Albie said.

She looked towards the stairway leading to downstairs. 'We need to leave, Dad.'

Albie brought her back to his room, making sure no one had seen them. 'Where would we go?'

'Somewhere,' Milly replied.

'This is somewhere,' he said. 'I can't afford to find another flat or even a room in a bedsit like this. I haven't even got a car.'

'We'll go on the train, or a bus. We'll go to a place in the countryside, like where we used to live.'

Albie looked at her. She looked at him.

'I'll protect you,' he said. 'I will kill anyone who threatens you. I won't risk losing you again. Not this time.'

Milly turned away from him and picked up her bear. 'That won't matter, if we stay here. If we stay here, you might as well kill me now.'

XVIII

CHAPTER EIGHTEEN

No one is going to hurt you, he had said to her, and he intended to keep his promise. They had spent the day in the room, watching cartoons and talking about old memories. He kept glancing at her, in both disbelief and joy, and couldn't believe she had returned.

Milly devoured the snacks from the kitchenette cupboard. Crisps and chocolate. Three cupcakes. Albie let her eat junk food because he loved her and couldn't stand to see her so thin and needy.

The day fell into dusk.

The rain did not cease, only worsened, and Albie stood at the window, observing the street outside while Milly sat on the bed and watched some old film on the small portable television he kept on a stool. The sound was low, barely a murmur. The rain thrashed against the building, turning the outside world to a watery ruin where car headlights glared past on the road. The pedestrians brave or foolish enough to risk going out into the downpour were no more than flitting shadows of vague menace on the pavements and in recessed doorways.

Thunder crackled in the distance, followed by a brief flash of lightning that filled the sky and imprinted afterglow stains upon Albie's vision. The hairs on his arms stiffened and his skin seemed to tighten, while neighbourhood dogs barked and fretted against the storm.

'I don't like the rain,' Milly said, out of nowhere.

He didn't move from the window. 'I know. Me neither. Do you remember much of that night in the village?'

She didn't answer immediately. 'It's all blurry, in bits and pieces. I remember Doctor Ridings taking me away to the other place.'

'I'm sorry I wasn't there,' Albie said.

'It's not your fault, Dad. You tried your best. There was nothing you could have done.'

The next two questions broke his heart to ask. He watched the rain, balling his hands into fists, blinking his eyes. 'Milly, did Doctor Ridings do anything to you? Did he…touch you?'

'I don't think he did,' she said. 'I don't think so.'

'You're sure? I won't be angry with you. It wouldn't be your fault.'

'I know, Dad.'

'It's going to be OK,' he said.

She just nodded.

Albie returned to watching the street. Adrenaline made him jittery and pensive. Creeping dread and fear swilled at the back of his mind, and acid frothed in his stomach, killing any pangs of hunger he might have felt after not eating all day.

A lone figure stood motionless on the pavement across the road, facing the bedsit. It was a thin, haggard shape dripping in the downpour. It was shadowed, murky and indistinct, as if Albie were viewing it through faulty eyes. And just before it faded away like some phantom passing out of this world, Albie was sure he'd glimpsed the flap of a white gown underneath a ragged coat.

He closed the curtains and stepped back from the window.

X

At some point during the night Albie woke from troubled dreams to find the door of his room open and Milly gone from the bed. He rose, groggy and unsteady, squinting in the dark. Streetlights from beyond the window defined the shapes of the room. His daughter was nowhere to be seen.

'Milly,' he said, and there was no answer, just silence inside the building and rain pattering on the window. He turned on the lamp then went out to the landing, where the sparse light from his room revealed no sign of her. Panic fluttered in his chest and warmed his face. He opened his mouth to breathe and looked down the stairway to the shadowed foyer at the entrance of the building, where he glimpsed Milly slipping through the wide doors to go outside. He called after her, called her name, but she didn't respond. He hurried down the stairs as the doors clanged shut and water pooled on the foyer floor.

Another call to her went unanswered, and he emerged outside into the driving rain, flinching and cringing, glancing around for her in the half-darkness of the street. Cars lined the kerbs either side of the road. The windows of the surrounding buildings and houses were darkened. There was no traffic at this late hour.

Milly was moving away to Albie's left, down the pavement towards the end of the deserted street. He staggered after her, splashing through oily puddles, reaching for her as if he was playing out a scene from a dream where he could never catch his daughter.

Lithe forms of shadow and knotted darkness, gesturing mockingly to him, were glimpsed in patches of streetlight on the other side of the road. A sound similar to the scraping of claws upon metal. He thought someone said his name in the rain, but ignored it and carried on, wiping his dripping face.

He stooped to recover Milly's toy bear from the pavement, and was gaining upon her, when several figures emerged from the darkness before her and stood gathered on the pavement. She halted, her hands motionless at her sides, facing the figures dressed in cowls or scraggly gowns. Their raw faces were partially visible within the hoods covering their heads.

Albie caught up with Milly and grabbed her right shoulder. She turned to face him and her eyes had gone to a pale pallor, bleaching her pupils, irises and corneas to dull white. Like a pallid film over her eyes.

Albie regarded the Flayed, facing them over a distance of twenty yards as they twitched and hunched over in their stained garments, like diseased vagrants seeking warmth and comfort.

'You can't have her back,' he said.

The Flayed said nothing. The man at the front of the group merely grinned, and his mouth moved with the suggestion of hunger.

When Albie looked down at Milly, her eyes had cleared and she stared at him in confusion and fear. 'What's happening, Dad?' Then she saw the Flayed and let out a little cry and stepped back against Albie, her shoulders shuddering in the cold and the rain.

'She doesn't belong to you,' the grinning man said, with the authority and eloquence of a true believer. 'She belongs to Doctor Ridings. As do we all. Even you, Albie. He let you live, back in the village on that glorious night. He looked inside your head and spared you. Now you are in his debt.'

'Fuck you,' Albie said. 'Leave us alone.'

The grinning man dismissed him with one shake of the head. 'That will not be possible, I'm afraid.'

Albie spat, held Milly against him. 'Whatever, dickhead. If Ridings touches her, I'll kill him.'

'Doctor Ridings is beyond death. He has…affiliates that are beyond your comprehension. You glimpsed their presence in the village, but your perception of them is like that of a flea in the company of leviathans. You will return the girl to us.'

'You'll have to come and get her. But I won't make it easy for you bastards.'

The man sighed, looked to the sky then back at Albie. He gave the impression of someone who was frustrated at having to deal with a person of much lower intelligence. He placed his hands together over his chest and glared at Albie, his eyes gleaming in the streetlight.

'Well, it would seem that tonight is your lucky night.' There was some humour in his voice. 'We've just returned, so we are lacking physical strength at the moment. But our *vigour* will soon return. And Doctor Ridings will return. You'd be wise to give your girl over to us before that happens. Doctor Ridings does not suffer fools.'

If Albie had a gun, he would have shot the man where he stood. He gritted his teeth and held the man's stare, and only when Milly pulled on his sleeve did he retreat with her in tow and hurry back up the street. When they reached the bedsit, Albie looked back, and the Flayed had disappeared back into the night in their stained cowls and hoods.

Back inside his room, he locked the door and placed the wooden chair underneath the handle to stop it from being turned. Milly was crying and trembling. He hugged her tightly, told her it would be all right and he would fix everything and never let her go again.

'What happened?' he asked her.

'They had some sort of control over me, because they're nearby and they know where I am. They were able to get inside my head. I couldn't fight them.'

'At least you're safe now.'

'We're not safe, Dad.'

He didn't reply.

Afterwards Milly took off her wet clothes and laid them on the radiator along with her sodden toy bear, then dried herself with a towel while Albie made hot chocolate. He made sure not to look at her before she slid under the bed sheets. And as she huddled with the drink cupped by her small hands, Albie went to the window and looked out at the street.

Languid figures and flailing forms beckoned to him from deep shadow and lightless alleyway mouths. Contorting shapes and faces of flesh reared and fell away in the darkness, like images from a dream. He glimpsed the vague coiling of a serpentine thing in the gutter. The streetlights flickered, and something wretched and clad in rags loped across the road and crouched with its hands busy at the blunt mound of its mouth.

He stepped back from the window and pulled the curtains closed. Then he went to the kitchenette and grabbed a carving knife from a drawer. The blade had lost its keen edge, but it was the best he could do, and it was better than facing a monster with bare hands and brave intentions.

X

He spent the rest of the night with the knife in one hand and his eyes flitting between the door and the first floor window. And during the night he went to the window and looked outside and saw several of the Flayed out in the street, watching in shadows away from the glare of the streetlights.

Milly slept and muttered, caught in dreams.

When dawn eventually broke over the grey street and lightened the sky in the east, the Flayed turned away and vanished into the side roads and narrow warrens of the town, like ghosts of memory.

XIX

CHAPTER NINETEEN

In the morning, after Milly had awoken and Albie sat groggy with lack of sleep, they agreed to leave and make for Kathleen's parents' house in Devon. He downed coffee and faced the wall while Milly dressed in her damp clothes. Afterwards they packed essentials and important items into a rucksack and two plastic bags. Albie made sure not to forget his photo album; to leave any photos or mementoes behind would have felt like betrayal. He gave one of the photos to Milly, as she had none of her own. It was a photo of her mother, taken while she was pregnant.

The girl looked as though she was going to cry. Her lower lip trembled, but did so with a smile that was wonderful on her pallid face. 'Thanks, Dad.'

'Take care of it,' Albie said.

'I will.' She put the photo in one tattered pocket of her coat.

Albie looked around the room. 'Luckily I'm not behind on the rent. I'll leave a note for the landlord. I don't think he'll be too bothered about me leaving without telling him. He turns over these rooms fairly quickly.'

'How much money do you have, Dad?' Milly asked. She appeared nervous, chewing on a fingernail. She wore an oversized jacket over her raggedy dress.

'We've got enough money to get us to your grandparents,' he said.

'What are we gonna tell them?'

'I expect they'll be glad to see you. I'll tell them the truth.'

'They'll want to know why I haven't gotten older.'

'I know. I'll tell them the truth.'

'And you'll tell them about Mum?'

'Of course. She was their daughter. They have a right to know.' There was a tremor in his voice as he thought of Kathleen. A swelling in his chest, full of grief, forced him to sit and close his eyes for a moment. And when he opened his eyes Milly was beside him and she put her arms around his shoulders and hugged him tight.

'I miss Mum,' she muttered. 'I miss our life before you and Mum divorced. I miss our old life and the village. I miss my friends.'

'I know,' he said. 'I miss it all.' And he hugged her back and it was their last moment of calm before they left the bedsit behind.

X

On their way to the train station, Albie took Milly to a charity shop and bought a bagful of clothes for her. The clothes smelled musty, but they were clean and in good condition. He found a pair of girl's boots with purple trim and Milly said she loved them despite being half a size too big for her. And she wore them without complaint.

She changed into her 'new' clothes behind a large bin in an alleyway while Albie stood with his back to her, keeping watch as the sounds of morning rush hour traffic rose from the surrounding streets and roads. Once that was done, Albie took her to a chemist's shop and bought her a toothbrush and other toiletries.

The sky was clouding over when they emerged back into the streets. He hoped the rain would stay away.

X

They moved through the busy streets, Albie watching for watchers, until they reached the train station. With most of Albie's remaining money they bought one-way tickets to Devon and waited on one of the platforms with their meagre bags and belongings. Dull specimens of people waited with them, mostly with their heads bowed to smartphones or magazines. Albie watched for the Flayed, one hand clenched into a fist by his side as he sat next to Milly on the bench at the back of the platform. She held his other hand and looked at him with a vague sadness. Perhaps it was melancholy. Albie couldn't tell, so he simply smiled a small smile at her and told her that the train would arrive soon.

X

They boarded the train and found seats at the end of the last carriage, away from other people and unwanted attention. He discreetly eyed the other passengers and appraised them. There seemed to be no threats on this particular carriage.

Milly was shivering as she watched the station recede behind them. She turned back to face the inside of the carriage, picking at her fingernails.

The bored voice of the driver droned over the speakers, notifying them of the stops awaiting them on the journey. Clatter and thump of the carriages upon the track. From somewhere ahead of Albie and Milly, a baby's cries faded to soft coos as it was soothed by its mother.

'Dad, do you think I'm real?' Milly said.

He looked at her. 'What sort of question is that? What do you mean?'

'You might be thinking that I'm not really your daughter. Do you think I am?'

Albie frowned at her. 'I think you're my daughter.'

'Really?'

'I *know* you're my daughter. There is no doubt in my mind. No doubt at all.' This wasn't entirely truthful, and he hoped it didn't show on his face. He hoped the small lie wasn't in his eyes. He had doubts, but had managed to push them to the back of his mind, along with the raw edges of sorrow he felt at Kathleen's death.

'What if I doubt it?' she said.

Albie hesitated, bit on the inside of his mouth. 'Do you?'

'I don't know.'

He went to put his hand on her arm, but held back at the last moment. 'I know you're my daughter. I don't think you're some doppelganger sent here to fool me. I know you're the same girl who was taken away from me five years ago.'

'What's a doppelganger?'

'It's an exact copy of someone, or something like that?'

'Okay.'

'Okay.'

'I missed you, Dad.'

'I missed you too,' he replied.

'And I miss Mum.'

'Go to sleep, Milly.'

'Don't you want to sleep? You didn't sleep much last night.'

'I'll be fine.'

'You sure, Dad?'

'Totally.'

'Okay.'

'Go to sleep.'

XX

CHAPTER TWENTY

Hours passed on the train. Milly slept with her face turned towards the rain-flecked window and her toy bear clasped in her arms.

Grey daylight, slowly fading to late afternoon. Shapes of towns and villages, like crude depictions upon the land. The countryside was indistinct as it rushed past the windows, and there were occasional figures standing in the fields, like ghosts or scarecrows. A mangled creature dwelled in an orchard, little more than a shadow amongst the trees. Albie glimpsed something tall and very thin lope alongside the tracks until the train left it behind. Then he looked to the dark sky and glimpsed the movement of an immense jellyfish-like form, all pale and writhing within the ashen folds of the clouds and skeins of rain, before the sky sealed itself anew and it was gone.

He heard sounds like shrill barking and bestial wailing and the keening of trapped animals, but it seemed like he was the only one to notice them. He screwed his eyes shut to the tortured cries from malformed mouths, gritted his teeth and bowed his head. It was a relief to hear the murmuring voices of people on the train. The baby's cries comforted him, offered hope in some insubstantial way, and when he opened his eyes Milly was awake and watching him. She asked if he was okay.

'I'm fine,' he said.

'You saw the monsters,' said Milly.

'Yeah.'

'It's okay, Dad.'

'I know. I'm all right.'

The girl sniffled. She always seemed so wan and tired and slightly distant, as if a part of her remained in the other place. 'I had bad dreams. Doctor Ridings spoke to me. Told me he'd find us wherever we ran. He said nowhere was safe.'

Albie felt his insides curdle. 'I'm sorry.'

'It's not your fault, Dad,' she said.

'I'll protect you, no matter what happens.'

'And I'll protect you.'

'I don't need protecting.'

'Yes, you do, Dad.'

X

They arrived at the last station on their journey and exited the train. Darkness in the sky and a cold wind bustling in the eaves of the roof over the platform. The rain had faded to an oily drizzle. They went out to the car park and waited for the bus to arrive, huddled together under the overhanging shelter on the pavement.

The train went on, disappearing down the tracks into the dark. People departed from the station in cars and taxis. An old woman shuffled past in a waterproof coat, dragging a wheeled suitcase behind her as she snorted and huffed with asthmatic breaths.

The bus arrived and parked next to the shelter. Milly shied away from its headlights and held Albie's hand. The pneumatic doors hissed open. They climbed the little steps onto the bus and paid the driver for their tickets then sat one row up from the backseats. They were the only passengers. The bus moved away, its exhaust chortling and belching, its insides smelling of stale sweat and vegetables left to decay. Albie didn't trust the damp patches on the floor.

Milly stared out the window and said nothing.

X

The bus driver kept glancing back at them from the rear-view mirror, wiping his mouth with one meaty paw. Albie didn't like the porcine characteristic of his damp, narrow eyes.

An hour later they arrived at the village. As Albie and Milly departed the bus, the driver merely grimaced at them to expose the neglect of his teeth. And then the bus left them behind in a gust of exhaust fumes. It was early evening, the sky sheer black with rainclouds, the drizzle cold and constant. Albie didn't like the mixture of villages and rain.

They looked around. The road was gleaming and slick, the street dull and dripping. This place wasn't even a village, more a hamlet of just over a dozen houses. It seemed to belong in the past. There was even a red telephone box, one of which he hadn't seen in years. The streetlights offered little against the darkness. The lights in the houses were pale yellow and unwelcoming, and Albie shivered, wringing his hands, his rucksack hooked over one shoulder. It all reminded him of Penbrook on that terrible night.

Milly huddled against him, squinting at the old buildings.

In the house directly across from them, a face appeared in an upstairs window and looked out at the new arrivals. Albie raised a hand in some sort of awkward greeting, but the person did not return it, so he lowered his hand and turned away.

They moved on, Albie leading the way. He kept hold of Milly's hand until they were clear of the houses and beyond the hamlet. He pulled out his torch to light the way as they walked the road that rose with the low hills. A short while later the squat shape of Kathleen's parents' converted farmhouse appeared out of the gloom upon the broad edge of a hill. The lights within the house were like signs guiding them to refuge.

Albie and Milly stopped at the entrance to the long, rising driveway and looked towards the house. A thin plume of smoke rising from the brick chimney. Albie had last been here almost eight years ago, and in the dark it seemed that nothing much had changed.

'I'm scared,' Milly said. 'What if they don't believe us?'

'Once they see you, they'll believe us. They'll believe the truth.'

'Okay.'

'Let's get this done.'

They went up the driveway, holding hands, slowly emerging into the lights thrown from the windows of the house.

CHAPTER TWENTY-ONE

The security light mounted against the nearest corner of the house lit them all the way to the front door.

They halted, shielding their eyes from the overhead glare, and regarded each other with anxiety and apprehension. Albie knocked three times on the front door and stepped back, keeping what he deemed a respectful distance from the threshold. The time between each heartbeat shortened and his stomach ached with nausea and hunger. Milly tensed beside him, her grip tightening on his hand.

They shivered in the drizzle.

The door opened. Stu Rawlins appeared in the doorway with his wife Cass standing behind, peering around his left shoulder. They looked at Albie with a displeasure that made him want to shrink away into the dark. He might as well have been a visiting leper in diseased rags. He might as well have been the one who killed Kathleen.

Despite their silent judgement and belligerence, he held his ground and looked back at them, shaking in his bones.

But then they saw Milly and their anger turned to shock, amazement and some kind of awe.

X

Albie and Milly sat beside each other at the kitchen table in the converted farmhouse. They still wore their coats. Cass watched them from her chair on the opposite side of the table, while Stu stood away from them all, waiting for the kettle to boil, glancing back over his shoulder at his granddaughter and former son-in-law.

The overhead lightbulb glimmered starkly. The walls were busy and cluttered with shelves of jars, ornaments and framed photos. Kathleen and Milly featured in most of the photos. There weren't any of Albie.

Cass laid her hands on the table top and cleared her throat. Opened her mouth a little. Albie felt an interrogation coming.

With barely restrained tension in his movements, Stu placed a glass of lemonade on the table for Milly. He looked at her like she wasn't real, before glancing at her toy bear on the table. His eyes appeared watery as he turned away to pour hot water into three mugs. Then he added milk and sugar to each one and handed them out.

Albie took his and sipped. It was good coffee, better than what he was used to. Stu drank from his own mug and remained standing, scratching absently at his beard with one hand. Cass left her coffee on the table. Steam rose from their drinks.

'Thanks,' Albie muttered, wilting under Cass and Stu's scrutiny. He looked at them, all the while wanting to look away.

'Explain this,' Cass said. She was a small, resolute woman who seemed shrunken inside her baggy sweater. 'Why is she alive? I thought they all died in the disaster?'

Albie wiped his mouth. And then he explained everything. He even told them about the village and the 'chemical spill' cover story concocted by the authorities, and how they'd forbidden him to divulge the real story to anyone. It didn't matter to him. Not now.

Stu and Cass listened. Milly drank her lemonade.

X

An hour later, Albie was finished and his throat was sore from talking. Stu and Cass just stared at him and Milly. Cass was in tears. Stu looked like he'd seen something awful. His hands were held to his not-inconsiderable stomach, and his face was bleached of colour.

'Is this a trick?' asked Cass. 'You're saying the government covered it all up? That when they said we couldn't see Kathleen and Milly's bodies because of the chemical contamination, they were lying?'

Albie exhaled. 'That's what I'm saying. It's not a trick.'

Cass looked at Milly. 'This isn't possible. She isn't dead. But she hasn't aged.'

Milly explained that part about the other place and how time moved much slower.

'And Kathleen is dead,' said Cass. 'How did she die?'

'A monster killed her in the spaces between the spaces,' said Milly. 'It happened quickly. She didn't know much about it.'

'But you survived, Milly. Somehow.'

'Yes.'

'This is madness,' muttered Stu, shaking his head and looking at the floor by his feet. 'Other dimensions and alien worlds? Gods and monsters?'

'I used to think it was madness, too,' Albie said. 'But you haven't seen the things I've seen.'

'Thin places,' said Milly.

Cass put down her coffee and glared at Albie. 'You've known what happened to Kathleen this whole time? You told us she was dead when there was a chance she wasn't. You lied to us.'

'I didn't know what happened to her. I just knew that she was taken. I wasn't allowed to tell you what I did know.'

'You bastard, Albie,' said Cass.

'I had no choice,' he said. 'The authorities made me sign an agreement. The government…'

'Fuck them all,' Cass snarled, veins thickening under the skin of her face. Her eyes were livid and pinkish around the edges. 'I hope they all die. And, you know, Albie, for the last five years I've been hoping you'd die. I prayed to God that you would die.'

'I'm sorry,' was all Albie could say. 'I'm sorry.'

'Please don't blame Dad,' Milly said. 'He didn't do anything wrong. It wasn't his fault; it was the fault of the bad people and the monsters.'

Albie wiped his mouth. 'I have no reason to lie to you both. Neither of us have a reason.'

'I don't know,' said Stu. He looked from Cass to Milly and appraised the girl. He stepped forward. 'Is it really you, Milly?'

'It's me, Grandad,' Milly said.

Stu stepped back, doubt and confusion across his face.

'Prove it,' said Cass, leaning forward at the table with her hands together. 'Prove that you're Milly and this isn't some kind of obscene prank.'

The girl frowned, thinking. Then she looked at Cass. 'I need to see my old room.'

X

Stu led them all upstairs to the room where Milly used to sleep when she visited. He opened the door and they went in, mindful of each other in the small room, whose walls had been recently decorated with fresh wallpaper. The bed was nothing but a bare mattress upon a metal frame. Albie could still smell the new paint.

Stu and Cass looked to Milly, and the girl went over to the far wall and crouched down in the corner, and with one fingernail scratched loose an edge of wallpaper and tore it upwards so that a ragged flap came free in her hands. And then she scraped away the underlying layers of paper and dried paste until she exposed something written on the cracked plaster. She stood and backed away, allowing the others to see.

Albie stepped forward with Stu and Cass either side of him. It was an inscription in dark ink, scratched by the hand of a little girl in the long ago.

My name is Milly Samways aged nine. I wish my parents would stop being mean to each other because it makes me sad and scared. I want to be an astronaut when I grow up.

'I remember writing that,' Milly said.

Cass began to cry. Stu put one hand to his face and stared at the words down in the corner of the wall. Albie glanced back at Milly, who stood there with her head lowered, her hands worrying at each other.

'Okay,' said Cass. She wiped her eyes, let out a tired breath, and looked at the girl. 'Okay.'

CHAPTER TWENTY-TWO

Albie stood on the sheltered doorstep at the front of the house, facing the darkened fields as he smoked a cigarette in the glow of the security lights.

After a while, he watched through the kitchen window as Milly ate baked beans on toast. Stu and Cass sat at either side of the table to her while she tore into the food with her knife and fork. There was talking and awkward laughter. Some warmth and light. Some comfort. Tentative kindness and restrained affection. They looked like family.

Milly had been accepted.

Albie smiled wanly in the slow drizzle then turned away and looked back out at the dark. There was a glimpse of the moon past the retreating rainclouds, and below that was patchwork farmland, serpentine roads, and the hamlet of old houses in the middle distance. Further out were the lights of towns and villages. He wondered if the Flayed were out there, searching for him and Milly.

He finished his cigarette and stamped it out on the ground. Just before he returned inside, the rain stopped and all was silent out in the dark. He listened for the cries and wailing of unearthly creatures, but there was nothing, and it gave him a small measure of peace.

X

Milly slept in her old room while Albie was given the other spare room at the back of the house. He undressed and lay under the blankets on an air mattress and stared at the ceiling in the dark, worrying that Milly might go sleepwalking.

But then he fell asleep and dreamed of Kathleen.

When he woke in the morning, he put his hand to his face and felt the trails of drying tears under his eyes.

X

The next day Albie and Stu walked the local fields while Cass and Milly stayed in the house. Albie was apprehensive about being away from Milly, but Stu promised they'd return within the hour. It was a day of overcast skies and no rain, with a bristling wind moving over the fields. The ground was damp and riddled with pools of dirty water.

'Did you sleep well?' asked Stu. He walked tall in his heavy coat, thick trousers and wellington boots. A woollen hat covered his balding scalp.

Beside him, Albie sniffled, hands in pockets, head bowed against the wind. 'Better than I've slept in a while.'

'Do you get bad dreams?'

'All the time.'

'Same here. Cass, too.'

Albie said nothing and kept walking. They were moving alongside an old stone wall that separated the field from the road. Damp dirt clung to his trainers. He was careful not to slip.

'We need to talk,' Stu said. He glanced at Albie with a concerned expression, the muscles tight within his face.

'About Milly,' said Albie.

There was a certain knowing in Stu's voice. 'About Milly, that's right.'

'Please don't tell anyone about her. Not the police or social services. Please don't, Stu.'

Stu halted and faced Albie, who eventually turned to look at him and stepped back, keeping his hands in the pockets of his coat. 'We have to tell someone, Albie. We can't just leave her to live like this, on the run and scared all the time. She has a life to live. She has to go to school.'

'I'll home school her,' said Albie, barely believing his own words.

Stu frowned, shook his head. 'She needs a proper life, with friends and homework and all the other things girls of her age have.'

'Other girls her age don't have mad people and monsters chasing after them.'

Stu exhaled through his mouth, looked across the field and then back to Albie. 'This…uh, cult you mentioned, led by some fucker called Doctor Ridings – it's very unlikely they'll find her here, isn't it? If that's the real story, of course.'

'You don't believe me?'

'I don't know what to believe, Albie. All I know is that my beloved granddaughter is back with us, and she has a chance at a real life. I've lost Kathleen, so Milly is all that me and Cass have left of our family.'

'You can't tell anyone, Stu,' said Albie. His arms were trembling.

'We don't have a choice,' Stu replied. 'She has to come back into society. We'll sort it all out.'

Something pressed on the back of Albie's eyes. His guts jangled and squirmed. The fear of losing Milly again formed a knot of sour nausea behind his diaphragm.

'I can't lose her again,' he said. 'If you tell the authorities, she'll be taken away and we will never see her again. She'll be experimented on. They'll run tests on her, cut her up like a lab rat, because she's the only person to return from another world. Do you want that to happen to your only granddaughter, Stu? Your little girl? You'd be responsible. And that's without even the cult being involved. Just be happy to have her back in our lives. Please don't take her away from me. I'm begging you. I've only just got her back.'

Stu stared down the field, indecision in his eyes. He wiped the patch of beard around his mouth and pursed his lips. He frowned at Albie but said nothing.

Albie told him: 'If you tell the authorities about Milly, I'll take her, and I promise you'll never see her again. I don't want to do that, but if you force me…'

Stu turned to face Albie and regarded him with a glimmer of anger in his eyes. His face darkened. 'I don't doubt you would. I know what kind of man you are.' The older man's shoulders shifted with his breathing. 'You bring Milly back to us then threaten to take her away again. You're not a good man, and you should be ashamed of yourself.'

Albie didn't flinch. 'I will do whatever it takes to protect my daughter. So, I suggest a truce between us. I know you and Cass have never liked me, even when Kathleen and me were together. You never thought I was good enough for her.'

There was no denial from Stu.

Albie continued: 'Can't we just make it work for Milly's sake?'

'And how will it work?' said Stu. 'Is Milly going to live here with me and Cass? Are *you* going to live here?'

'I don't know,' Albie said. 'I'll think of something. But for now, all we need is shelter, and no interference from the authorities. I won't let her get taken away.'

'But you'll take her away, if you have to?'

'I will.'

'You're a piece of shit.'

'I can live with that.'

Stu sighed. 'Fair enough.'

'Truce?'

'Yes. Let's keep walking.'

CHAPTER TWENTY-THREE

They ate a dinner of sausages, chips and peas around the kitchen table while the last of the light faded and rain fell at the windows.

The food was delicious, but Albie's appetite wasn't what it used to be, and he picked at the chips with his fork and placed them into his mouth and chewed slowly. There was water and lemonade to drink. Conversation was sporadic and awkward, and whenever Albie looked at Cass, he caught her glaring back at him before she turned her head away. Her eyes were livid with frustration and a seething anger that she was barely keeping a lid on. Stu appeared apologetic and glum, absently pushing his food around his plate as he looked down at the table.

Albie didn't care that Stu had told her about their conversation that morning. He appreciated and respected their feelings on the matter, but Milly's safety was all he cared about. Nothing else mattered.

He'd expected Cass to launch some sort of tirade at him, but nothing came, and when the meal was finished there was only silence as they all looked at one another, waiting for someone to say something.

Cass took the plates from the table and started piling the washing up in the sink. Stu went to help her. Milly looked at Albie and offered a sad smile.

X

It was past nine pm when Milly went to bed and Albie accompanied her to make sure she brushed her teeth. When she was done in the bathroom, they went to her room and talked about the old days and her mother. Then they spoke about the future.

'I don't know what's going to happen,' Albie said. 'But I'll always be here for you, no matter what happens.'

'I know, Dad,' Milly said.

'Things will work out in the end.'

'Yeah, Dad.'

The door opened and Cass entered the room with a steaming mug of something. She smiled at Milly and ignored Albie. She placed the mug on the bedside table. A faint smell of cinnamon rose from the drink.

'Warm milk,' Cass said to Milly. 'It'll help you sleep, my dear. Make sure you drink it before it goes cold.'

'Yes, Nan,' Milly said.

'We'll let you get to bed.' Cass said. 'You need your rest.' She hugged Milly and kissed her forehead, then turned away without so much as glancing at Albie.

He kissed Milly goodnight and followed Cass out of the bedroom. He closed the door and stood in the corridor, then tried to talk to Cass, but she was already walking away.

X

A short while later, tired and aching, he went to bed and lay in the soft light of his bedside lamp, staring at a photo of the family he used to have.

He fell asleep pining for Kathleen and the old times, and dreamed of places beyond any earthly hue, where the hellish cries of tortured men and women echoed and reared like the sound of animals led to slaughter.

X

He woke to grey morning light and stumbled out of bed to find he couldn't open the door of his room. He banged on the door and rattled the handle, calling for someone to let him out. He called for Milly. But he already knew, deep down in his gut, what had happened.

Moments later he kicked the door open and staggered into the corridor between the landing and the bathroom, then rushed into Milly's room and found her bed unmade and the photo album left open upon the crumpled sheets. He stood there, breathing hard through his teeth, swallowing lumps in his throat. He could still smell her. Some of her clothes had been taken. The photo he'd given her was gone. The bed was cold when he placed his hand upon it, and it was all he could do not to break down and slump to his knees like a man at the end of it all.

The other upstairs rooms were deserted. Rain tapped upon the roof.

He hurried downstairs and clattered through the rooms. He went outside and walked around the house, oblivious to the downpour. The car was gone from the driveway.

A note had been left on the kitchen table.

Blinking tears from his eyes, biting down on panic and seething dread and trembling fury, he read the note:

We couldn't let you take her away. She deserves a real life, away from your madness. She deserves a chance to be happy. If you love her and want the best for her, you'll leave her alone. Let her go, Albie.

He tore the note into several pieces and let them flutter down to the floor. The edges of his vision whitened, his face grew hot, and his knuckles cracked as he made fists out of his hands and realised he'd lost Milly again, this time for good. He slumped against the table and cried, put his hands to his face and dug his fingers into the skin until the pain was too much and there was blood under his nails. He shouted his daughter's name, his voice fading to choking sobs before he flipped the table over, sending plates and bowls crashing to the floor. A vase of flowers shattered.

He collapsed to his knees, devastated and wordless, keening in his throat, pounding his hands on the floor until his palms were raw and all rational thought had abandoned his mind to leave a white-hot core of anger raging in his fragile heart.

PART
THREE

XXIV

CHAPTER TWENTY-FOUR

Six hours earlier.

Milly woke disorientated and thirsty in the half-darkness, and took a few moments to realise she was lying across the backseat of Grandad's car. Her toy bear was in her arms.

Beyond the windows was nothing but night and rain. She sat up, her head aching, the inside of her skull numb and her thoughts sluggish. She rubbed her face and looked about, wincing at the chemical taste in her mouth.

Nan and Grandad sat in the front of the car. There was no sign of her father. Grandad was driving, facing straight ahead as the wipers struggled to keep away the heavy rain. The road ahead was deserted, without traffic, like a depthless dark save for the headlights thrown by the car. She felt as if they were moving through an abyss. In the rear view mirror, Grandad's face appeared severely pale and his shadowed eyes were squinting out at the downpour. He glanced back at Milly with something like alarm and shame.

'Cass,' Grandad said to Nan. 'She's awake.'

Milly sat there, fighting the vagueness inside her head. She put one hand to her heaving stomach. 'Where's Dad? What's happening?'

Nan looked back at Milly, half-turning in her seat. 'We're taking you to a safe place, my dear. Somewhere where you'll be taken care of.'

'Where?' Panic fluttered in her guts. The racing of her heart made her feel sick.

'A police station,' Nan said, almost apologetic. 'Don't worry, we'll stay with you. No one's going to hurt you.'

'A police station? But I haven't done anything wrong.'

'We're going there for your own protection. From your father. We need to report what's happened.'

'Where's my dad?' she asked, breathing harshly through her nose. 'Tell me where he is.'

A moment of hesitation as Nan sighed. 'We left him behind. We left him sleeping. He's become unstable, with all this talk of monsters and other dimensions. He's lost his mind and somehow gotten you to go along with it. He's not safe to be around, Milly. He's unhinged.'

'Don't talk about him like that,' Milly said.

'We gave you a crushed up sleeping pill in your warm milk,' Grandad said. 'We disguised the taste with some cinnamon. There was no other choice, love.'

'No other choice,' Nan muttered. 'We had to do it.'

'You can't do this,' Milly said. 'You can't take me away from my dad.'

'He's gone mad,' Nan replied. 'Making up all these stories and stuff. It's not normal and he needs help. He's not right in the head.'

'It's all true, I promise.'

'You don't have to stick up for him anymore,' said Grandad. 'It's OK. You don't have to lie for him ever again.'

'Take me back to the house,' Milly said. 'Please. Please take me back to see him.'

'We can't do that,' said Nan. 'I'm sorry.'

'You'll see him again, when he's better,' Grandad told Milly.

Nan looked at Grandad as if he'd said something stupid and untrue.

A sob stuck in Milly's throat. She wanted to scream, but there was no strength in her lungs and her limbs felt drained and useless. 'I didn't even get to say goodbye to him.'

'Everything's going to be fine,' said Nan, looking back at her. 'We're not going to leave you, Milly. I promise. It's going to be all right.'

Milly thought of Doctor Ridings and the Flayed, and shook her head as she stared out her window. Something was coming. Something made of darkness.

'No, it won't be,' she said. 'It really won't be.'

The attack happened fast.

Grandad was the first to cry out as the large, writhing shape of swarming tendrils rushed out of the dark from the right side of the road, barely glimpsed in the limits of the headlights.

There was nothing to be done.

The car was struck on the driver's side by a great weight similar to that of a truck or large van and was slammed towards the roadside. The shrieking of metal mixed with Nan's screams as glass shattered. Grandad threw his hands to his face. Milly watched, aghast, as the roof bent inwards from something pressing down on the car. The sheer bulk of the thrashing thing blocked the headlights and filled the windows with squirming black flesh.

This creature was the Wraith, and it had been searching for her.

Milly didn't scream.

Not when the shrill wail of the beast echoed in the rain, and multiple, glowing white eyes of burning light came to the windows to peer in at the trapped prey.

Not even when the car was lifted several feet from the tarmac and thrown into the ditch at the roadside.

And there was brief vertigo, her insides juddering, then the awful smash and tearing of impact, and finally nothing but a terrible silence. Until the silence was broken by the damp slither and scrape of the creature's tendrils entering through the car's broken windows.

CHAPTER TWENTY-FIVE

Albie went outside the house and stood in the rain, slumping like a drunk, holding his hands to his face as he looked out at the grey fields. The sound of thunder tolled in the sky. A ringing, much like tinnitus, filled his ears, and when he took his hands from his face he noticed movement some distance away in his peripheral vision.

He turned to see several of the Flayed watching from the half-shadows beneath the spiked boughs of bare trees.

The sight of them sent prickling along the back of his arms. The breath caught in his throat and he stepped back towards the house as the shrouded figures began making their way across the fields towards him.

More of the Flayed appeared closer to him, filthy and ragged, as if they'd risen from the porous mud to beseech him with their skinned faces and the hooked blades in their hands.

Albie staggered inside the house and locked the door.

X

He tried to escape through the back of the house, but when he reached the rear door and looked out through the small window next to it, more of the Flayed were standing in the back garden, waiting for him to emerge. They were like scarecrows in the rain, glaring at him from within their cloth hoods and robes. He locked the back door and retreated towards the middle of the house, halting in the narrow corridor outside the living room, breathing hard, his legs watery and weak. He leaned against the wall in full sight of the front door. Closing his eyes for a second, he stifled a sob and thought this would be the end of it all, and he remembered that moment in the church in Penbrook, on that terrible night, when he'd been given some kind of strange mercy by Doctor Ridings and his followers.

The front door began to open. He'd locked it, but that didn't seem to matter anymore. He shook his head and bit down on a hysterical laugh.

Doctor Ridings stepped into the house, and he was much as Albie remembered him – the bronze mask, wisps of yellowing hair flailing from its sides like a sickly mane. And the pale eyes, cruel and damp, were visible through the holes in the mask. Ridings' robes of dull white were seemingly untouched by the rain. He was a grand figure, a man who'd walked between worlds and witnessed gods die. He'd seen the fate of all life. Albie knew this, and almost admired him.

'I know you,' Albie said. 'I see you.'

CHAPTER TWENTY-SIX

Milly's grandparents were unconscious when the slick tendrils wrapped around them and pulled their prone bodies out of the wrecked car. Their seatbelts had been ripped away. Only once they were outside did Milly hear them struggle and groan, their sounds slowly muffled and muted, followed by the cracking of their bones.

She was lying on her side, dazed and shaken, shivering with shock, seeing the world through tears and encrusted blood from the gash on her forehead. Moving slowly, carefully, mindful of any other wounds upon her, she crawled out of the side of the car away from the road and into the hedgerow, burrowing and pawing like an animal, waiting for the tendrils to latch onto her leg. Rain fell in the vegetation. Brambles scratched at her bare skin and snagged her clothes. And she was already in the wet meadow on the other side before she even realised she'd escaped. She cried for her grandparents and hoped they died without knowing much about it. They had died for their misguided good intentions. They had taken her away from her father, but she couldn't hate them for it. And she would mourn them, but not yet.

She crawled. Sopping grass soaked her and the rain fell into her eyes. She moved forward blindly, groping in a direction she thought would take her away from the road. Bristles and keen edges of grass cut her hands, arms, knees, legs. Insects and small mammals moved in the undergrowth, scurrying away from her. A beetle flitted across her face. In the distance, something rang out, like the pealing of a church bell. But then it was gone and she didn't hear it again. Larger things skittered through the meadow around her, and she prayed she would not be found. Monsters called to her from the road, imitating the voices of her grandparents. She would not be fooled.

She went on.

The meadow thinned, became scrubland, and she rose to a crouch and stopped and listened. Ahead of her, a stretch of woodland was all shadow and tall shapes. It would offer shelter.

Milly moved in a hunched, hobbling run, and when she reached the woods she realised that she'd left her toy bear behind. A pang of sadness ached within her as she was swallowed by the trees.

X

Moving though the woodland, gasping and grieving, Milly kicked through mulch, dirt and nests of toadstools. The air smelled fungal and overripe, scented with corruption. Something giggled from over her left shoulder, but when she looked back there was nothing.

The thin places were becoming thinner.

X

She emerged from the woods and climbed over a low, crumbling stone wall. On the other side of the wall was a derelict graveyard and in its centre a ruined chapel. She stood still, regaining her breath, placing her hands to the scrapes, cuts and welts she'd suffered during the crash and her escape through the meadow and the woods.

She walked amongst the graves as the rain fell. Forgotten names on time-ravaged and weathered headstones. Some of the names had been worn away. The grass was overgrown, riddled with flourishing weeds and brambles. She picked her way carefully until she was at the ancient doorway of the chapel. The door itself was long gone, unscrewed from its hinges in the long ago. Darkness beyond the doorway, but it smelled dry, and she needed to get out of the rain.

She stepped inside and felt her way along a stone wall. Her feet scraped on rough flagstones coated with gravel and dust. Something small flapped past her face in the dark, leaving a pungent reek of dung and musty skin. She did not cry out and did not scream, for she had encountered fiercer creatures than bats in places far worse than this. She had been in the presence of gods and survived to dream about it.

Eventually she found a dry corner and sat down with her knees drawn to her chest, shuddering and sniffling in the scattering of brick fragments and dusty cloth. Most of the roof was gone, affording her a view of the black sky. No stars. But she was out of the rain, at least, and the sound of distant traffic comforted her.

She didn't sleep for the rest of the night.

CHAPTER TWENTY-SEVEN

Albie wasn't sure when he'd properly awakened and become aware of his surroundings. A darkened room with damp walls of red brick and a bare plaster ceiling. No windows. One door without a handle twenty yards ahead of him. Some sort of basement, maybe, with a bare cement floor covered in dust and grit. Beyond the surrounding walls rose the faint sound of singing – funeral hymns, solemn prayers, and low chanting.

He sagged and groaned on his knees, with his hands tied at his back with rope and attached to a metal bracket on the wall behind him. He bowed his head until his chin rested upon his chest, and tried to work saliva into his mouth, which tasted of his own blood. His dry throat pained him, and the craving for water brought him to despair. His entire body was wracked with sharp aches that seemed to burn deep inside his muscles. The rope chafed at his wrists and his knees were sore. It was hard to gather his thoughts. His last memory was of being dragged away from Stu and Cass's house by chattering men in filthy robes and cowls. He recalled shrill voices muttering his name, stifling laughter and mirth, and a glimpse of skinless faces.

The sound of shoes scraping nearby over the floor caused him to raise his head. And he looked up to see Doctor Ridings standing in front of him, a grand sight in holy robes and the bronze mask. White silk gloves covered his thin hands. His damp mouth opened, took in a breath, and displayed the browning teeth clotted with what looked like tuna meat. He smelled of dead flowers.

'Why haven't you killed me?' Albie said.

Ridings scrutinized him through the bronze mask. Then the man finally spoke, and his voice was rasping and thick with dampness. Saliva speckled his scabbed, tattered lips.

'I had plans for you, Infidel. You were supposed to tell the world about me and the other places. You were supposed to be my witness – that's why I spared your life that night in the village.' He gave a long wheeze that rattled in his throat and sunk into his chest. 'But you have displeased me, Infidel. You hid yourself away, denied the sacred task I had given to you. I blessed you, sent you forth to prepare the way, but you failed me. But I have another task for you, because now you will help me find your little girl.'

It hurt Albie to gather air into his lungs. Garbled voices scraped inside his head. Something tittered from within one of the walls. 'Her grandparents took her. I don't know where she is.'

'My Wraith took care of her grandparents. The girl escaped.'

'Stu and Cass are dead?'

'Was that their names?'

'Yes.'

'They're dead. My Wraith consumed them.'

Albie sagged, stifled a sob. 'Why do you want her?'

'Didn't she tell you, Infidel?'

'She couldn't remember.'

Ridings scoffed from behind his mask. 'She carries my child.' There was a note of victory in his voice.

The air seemed to waver in front of Albie's eyes. His throat tightened with anger and disbelief. A pressure building in his skull. It felt like the world was ending. And he tried to pull on the rope holding him to the wall, to get at Ridings, to bite him with the only weapon he had left, until he fell back to his knees when his strength failed him.

'You mean, you…' He screwed his eyes shut, then opened them to Ridings' grinning mouth. 'You and her…'

Ridings said, 'She had no choice, if it helps. But in the end she was quite welcoming.'

'I'm going to kill you,' said Albie. 'Whatever it takes. I'll smash your head in. I'll rip your fucking heart out.'

Ridings reached out with one silk-gloved hand and patted the top of Albie's head. He ruffled his hair. Albie tried to pull back, but Ridings grasped a handful and held him in place. Then he withdrew the hand into his robes.

Trembling with anger, Albie caught a glimpse of the man's wrist, all jaundiced and ravaged with lesions and vivid veins.

Ridings sighed, and Albie couldn't tell if it was a pleasurable or tired sound. 'It's not as abhorrent as you think, Infidel. In olden times it was completely acceptable. And, like you said, she doesn't even remember. Luckily for her. But *I* remember.'

White hot rage broiled beneath Albie's skin. His pulse barely had space between each beat. Fury whitened his vision. He was trembling all over, clenching his teeth until his skull filled with a high-pitched ringing. Prickly heat covered his face, tempting him to scratch at the skin and rip it all away.

'You'll be punished for this,' said Albie, meeting Ridings' eyes above him. 'I swear to God.'

Ridings shrugged, glanced towards the ceiling, and held out his arms at his sides. 'God's not here. God's not anywhere. Even if he was real, there are older things out there. Things with more power than Yahweh, Allah, or any pagan god. Things that would make your God look like a child. But it's going to work out for you, Infidel. You can have your daughter back, when she's served her purpose. Once she's given birth, you can take back whatever remains of her.'

'Given birth?' Albie said, with such horror that his voice failed and he could only whimper.

'Yes. She will give me a child. A glorious child.'

'No,' Albie muttered. He was crying and groaning, witless with his suffering. 'You're not going to hurt her.'

'I've already hurt her, as I've just told you.'

'Fuck you.'

Ridings' eyes remained cold and without fear of any retribution Albie could enact. 'I just need your help, Infidel. Don't you want to see her again? We have a common goal, from what I can see. The Wraith is out there, searching for her, and with your help she'll come back to us soon enough.'

'I won't help you,' Albie said. 'I'd rather she remained lost than return to you and suffer again.'

'We're all suffering,' said Ridings. He crouched and leaned in close. His breath was sulphurous and rotten. 'Existence is suffering. But suffering can be magnificent.'

Albie flinched as Ridings began stroking his hair. A damp smile filled the mouth hole in the mask. 'I forgive you, Infidel.' And Ridings withdrew his hand and slowly removed his mask, laid it on the floor and looked at Albie, who tried to back away but found it impossible.

Ridings' face was a ruin of dry tumours and pustules, shockingly white, the skin stretched taut over his angular cheekbones and around his eyes, like a desiccated mask of scar tissue and knotted epidermal layers. His chin was slight and soft above the sagging jowls of his throat. Ridings leaned in close, as if for a kiss, and opened his papery mouth to reveal a thick writhing appendage of pale flesh that shot between Albie's open jaws and down his throat, choking him into manic shock and hysteria.

Ridings' voice spoke inside Albie's head as he offered communion.

I forgive you, Infidel. I forgive you and bless you. Be at peace in your suffering.

CHAPTER TWENTY-EIGHT

When the first smears of light defined the eastern horizon, Milly went outside yawning and rubbing at her stinging eyes. She looked around. Her stomach cramped with hunger and thirst worried at the back of her mouth. Her legs were stiff from sitting on the stone floor all night. Exhaustion made her thoughts hazy and filled her head with worry. She was tempted to stay in the chapel and rest, but then realised she had to keep moving in order to escape the Wraith.

Before leaving she crouched on the dewy grass amongst the ancient gravestones and remembered her grandparents and her father and wept for them. There was only silence.

She was alone and lost, a slumped form in cast-offs from an Oxfam shop.

X

She meandered down a lane hemmed in by tall conifers and shadows. She held her hands to her aching stomach, glancing behind to check she wasn't being followed. The trees fell away and the lane continued between furrowed fields. The land dipped ahead of her, revealing a shallow valley, with houses dotted amongst the fields and hillocks. There were villages and towns further on, while to the east cars travelled a road on the higher ground, sunlight glinting from their windows. She wondered about the lives of the people in the cars and if they were happy. She wondered if monsters were chasing them, and she almost laughed.

Farther on, she stopped and crouched before a colony of small mushrooms at one side of the lane. She leaned forward and sniffed at them. No smell. Glistening black and dirty brown. They looked diseased. She picked one, the stem snapping from the dirt, and it crumbled in her hand to leave an oily stain on her palm. She looked down at the other specimens and decided not to risk it. Better to be hungry than poisoned and sick.

She wiped her hand on the grass then moved on.

X

Milly walked and stumbled, holding her head to endure the visions she suffered. The things she saw brought her to tears, had her muttering into her hands, and forced her to lean against trees and fence posts.

She saw a vision of the Flayed standing in a distant field on a broad hillside. They were staring at the sky, arms raised from the husks of their dilapidated bodies within the shrouds of their filthy cowls and gowns. She looked away then looked back to them, and they were gone. She thought her father had been amongst them, desperately calling out to her, waving his hands as if he was struggling to stay afloat in deep water.

More visions came in the rain that followed, of her time in the other places of chaos and boundless dark. She shuddered, biting on the knuckles of one hand, her eyes bulging in the holes of her skull.

She tasted blood and swallowed it.

Skeletal horses running in clouds of ash and distant lightning. A hundred naked bodies impaled and twitching on tall black spikes. Men with their skin torn away, blood spilling from their gibbering mouths, holding their scalps in their hands. Serpentine beasts writhing below a red sun in a red sky. Leviathans rising from abyssal depths in the starless dark. Meat and murder. Echoes of death and desperate cries from glistening alcoves of alien resin. The black star. Abominations, blind and immense, worshipped by the weak spawn that suckled on their teats. Idiot gods tittering in the lightless void. Men and women stumbling through the dark, only to be snatched away and devoured by terrible things with leathery wings and mouths of busy tentacles.

Stinking spaces, caverns of rot, sopping intestines and piles of viscera, amongst which crimson worms burrowed and gnawed. The drooping udders of a mother creature. Doctor Ridings' voice as he prayed in the putrid chambers of flesh worship. And something beyond comprehension reached out and blessed him. His prayers were answered and he was transformed, augmented, hollowed out and given the greatest of gifts.

X

She came to standing in the middle of the lane, swaying on her feet with the fields and dense thickets around her. Thunder far away in the sky. She had no idea how far she'd walked during her visions. The lay of the land seemed similar to before, but she couldn't be sure.

But she was certain someone had been standing behind her – until she turned and saw no one there. The treetops rustled in the wind. Some small mammal flitted through the scrub, darting away. Gooseflesh rose on the backs of her arms.

At first she thought the discomfort in her stomach was hunger, but when it bloomed into something more she fell to her knees and the pain was deep with sharp fingers in her abdomen. She collapsed to one side, whimpering, eyes streaming, rigid with the agony inside her.

She thought she heard a baby wail from somewhere in the distance, but it was a ghostly and animalistic sound not from any human mouth.

She blacked out, the world fading away for a moment, and when it returned a man with a simple face and dull eyes stood gazing down at her with vague confusion and interest.

XXIX

CHAPTER TWENTY-NINE

The man carried her in his arms to a campsite of old caravans and rusting machinery situated upon an expanse of wasteland. Dogs barked and children clamoured, chattering around the man as he walked. Feet kicked and splashed through mud. The man's laboured breathing warmed her left ear. He smelled of wood varnish and salty sweat, and his body was large and soft around her.

Men were talking nearby. Raised voices in rough, broad accents. The man ignored them and took Milly to a caravan near the centre of the campsite. The door to the caravan opened and an old woman stepped outside, hunched in a woollen shawl and scarves of thin cloth over a tattered cardigan. A long, wide skirt covered her legs. Her face was kindly but creased, with a hardness in her eyes from troubled times. She looked at the man and gestured for them to come inside, and once they entered she followed and closed the door. The watching children were left outside.

X

The inside of the caravan smelled of lavender and liniment. The man had laid Milly down on a faded couch decorated with the patterns of flowers. Two bars of a gas fire burned. Trinkets and porcelain figurines of angels adorned shelves and decorative tables. Commemorative plates for royal marriages were aligned along a Welsh dresser. Sepia-stained photos in frames featured long-dead people – workers in hayfields and men toiling in the soil of some farmland. Portraits of ghosts. A boy and his dog stood beside a river in a photo dated *1963*.

The air was thick and warm, like treacle, and lulled her to the edge of sleep, but she didn't give in, and rubbed at her eyes and sat up. The pain was fading from her stomach, but she grimaced with hunger-nausea and took deep breaths. She couldn't speak. Weakness softened her limbs.

The old woman gave Milly sweet tea, and then a bowl of a vegetable soup with two slices of buttered bread. She sat in the armchair across from Milly and watched her eat, twiddling with her thumb and forefinger the small silver cross hung around her neck. When Milly was done, the woman put the crockery in the kitchenette sink and returned to the armchair. She looked at Milly, the fingers of one hand tapping on the table surface near a stack of romance novels.

'You're lost,' the woman said. 'But you're safe here. What's your name?'

Milly gave her name.

The woman nodded, as if Milly had given a correct answer. 'I'm Esme. My son, Bryn, brought you back here. He's in his room working on his airplane models. He won't be out for a while.'

Milly wiped her mouth and said nothing.

'Your clothes are filthy,' said Esme, eyeing the baggy jumper. 'Did you run away from home?'

Milly sniffled, scratched one side of her face and tried not to look away when she told her lie. 'I'm an orphan. I ran away from my foster home.' She left it at that, and she knew that Esme didn't believe her.

The old woman frowned, glanced at Milly's stomach. Milly swallowed down the tender lining of her throat.

'You can stay here for a while,' said Esme.

'Thank you,' Milly replied, one hand absently rubbing her belly, which seemed overly swollen from such little food.

XXX

CHAPTER THIRTY

Not long after midday, Esme took Milly on a walk around the campsite. Bryn traipsed behind them, muttering to himself and gazing at the ground. The caravans formed a vague ring around a wide clearing where a makeshift shed sagged amongst the wrecks of obsolete machinery. Gas canisters stood against one outer wall of the shed. People stood in the doorways of their caravans or outside them. Others worked at physical tasks, cutting wood, fixing furniture, or hanging washing on wire lines. Most of them glanced at Milly, offering curt looks, but they said nothing.

She noticed a few scarred faces amongst them. A woman with severely tied-back hair held her left arm in a sling. Two heavily-bearded men stood together, passing a cigarette between them, and stared at Milly until she passed.

Someone was singing lowly from a nearby caravan. A soft, wavering melody. It sounded like an old folk song.

The ground was patchy with yellowed grass, dirt and mud, and crumpled with shoeprints. A group of children kicked a football around and pretended not to watch Milly. The children were ragged things, all skinny and rangy, with suspicious eyes and scruffy hair. They wore t-shirts and tracksuit bottoms or frayed jeans.

Near one end of the site, several mangy dogs paced and barked in kennels. Nearby, a campfire burned, tended by a woman in a denim jacket. She stared at the flames. Wood smoke drifted in a thin plume, taken by the breeze.

They halted at the edge of the camp, where the wasteland was infested with weeds and brambles. Burnt patches of ground. Scattered trash and smashed bottles. Shards of green glass. A pile of black bin bags swollen by their insides, some of them torn, dripping stinking fluids and juices. Broken toys, and a metal bucket losing itself to rust.

'We make the best of what we've got,' Esme said.

Milly was reluctant to stand too close to the woman. 'How long have you been here?'

'A long time. Since before Bryn was born.'

'He's your son?' Milly glanced back at Bryn, who was staring vacantly at the birds flitting about the distant trees away to their left.

'Yes,' Esme said. 'His father died years ago. Got killed in a fight.'

'I'm sorry.'

'It's all right. My husband was a bad man. I don't miss him, and Bryn was only a baby. He has no memory of him.'

'I can't stay here,' Milly said. 'I can't risk staying here.'

Esme looked at her, eyes narrowing. 'You're being chased.'

Milly nodded.

'I know you lied to me about running away from the foster home.'

Milly said nothing.

'Who is chasing you?' Esme asked.

'You don't want to know.'

'The police? Social services? You're in trouble with the law?'

'Much worse, I'm afraid. Bad people.'

'Why are they chasing you?'

Milly shrugged, turned to appraise the scrubland and dilapidation before them. 'I'm not even sure anymore.'

Esme stepped closer to Milly and folded her arms, her grey hair ruffled by the breeze. The laughter-lines around her eyes were deep. She pursed her mouth before speaking. 'Something's wrong with you, Milly.' She paused, exhaled, bit on her lower lip. 'Sometimes I just know things.'

Milly regarded the silver cross around Esme's neck. 'Did your god tell you?'

'In a way,' said Esme.

'What does that mean?'

'God gave me a gift that lets me look into a part of other people. I can see their dreams. I can see their memories. Even their hidden memories, the things they've forgotten.'

'And your gift told you that something's wrong with me?'

'Yes.' Esme took a breath, seemed to prepare her next words carefully. 'I think that the Devil laid his hands upon you and tried to claim you as one of his own.'

Milly stepped away.

Esme smiled a pained smile. 'It's all right, Milly, I'll look after you. I'll take care of you. I will stop the Devil from taking your soul.'

CHAPTER THIRTY-ONE

Milly, Esme and Bryn had eaten a dinner of pork chops, chips and runner beans at the small dining table while darkness fell outside and lights and lamps flared on inside the other caravans. Afterwards, Esme made Milly sit with her and Bryn on the sofa and watch old black-and-white films. Esme kept saying that she would look after Milly. But Milly only wanted to get away.

She decided to leave after Esme and Bryn had gone to sleep. So, she waited, and then noticed that the swelling of her stomach had not gone down.

X

She'd been given the couch to sleep on, and a soft blanket to keep her warm. And a few hours after Esme and Bryn had retired to their rooms, most of it spent lying on her back in the darkness and staring at the ceiling, she lifted the blanket aside and rose from the couch, moving as quietly as possible. The floor gave a soft creak and she winced. She pulled on her coat and her shoes then crept towards the door to leave, but before she reached it Esme's voice rose from behind her, stopping her in place.

'I knew you would do this.'

Milly tensed and sucked in a breath that caught in her chest and swelled her lungs. A smear of light from beyond the window fell across her face. She turned around and faced the dark, which shifted away in the flare of an LED lantern and revealed Esme's impassive face.

'I have to go,' Milly said. 'You've been very kind to me, but I can't stay here. I'm sorry.'

Esme rose from the armchair. She was shaking her head, and her eyes were sad. 'You can't leave until we help you. You can't leave until we banish the Devil from your heart.'

The door of the caravan opened and men with torches entered and grabbed Milly. She struggled, begged to be released, but her pleas were met with silence, and they took her outside and showed her where she would be saved. Esme was talking behind her, offering words of comfort and promises of salvation, and more of the camp's inhabitants emerged from their homes to help in the glow of the bonfire that was suddenly ignited. The flames grew and reached and thickened, and the heat scratched upon Milly's skin and made her cry. The travellers gathered around her. Even the children were there, watching in silence with their parents and older siblings.

'You will be saved,' said Esme, placing one hand on Milly's shoulder. 'You will be saved and allowed into Heaven and you should be grateful.'

An old man, eyes wide, mouth fixed into a lipless sneer, pointed at Milly's distended stomach with one bony finger. 'Look at her!'

Several murmurs rose from the crowd.

Milly turned her face away from him and lowered her head, looking down at her belly. It might have been a trick of the light, but she'd sworn something had rippled under the skin of her stomach. She shook her head and tried to deny it, tried to ignore the feeling of writhing movement within her.

'It's time,' Esme said from behind her.

The men forced Milly to her knees in the dirt and pulled her coat from her shoulders. When she tried to resist and thrash in the men's arms, one of them slapped her hard across the face to leave her cheek stinging. Her head drooped, and the world went distant, indistinct and thudding for a few moments. A light rain began to fall. Her head cleared to the low recital of Bible verses, sacred scripture and holy words.

'I'm sorry,' Esme said to her. 'This is for your own good.'

Milly didn't reply, and said nothing when the back of her jumper was lifted, exposing bare skin. A calloused hand touched the small of her back. She shivered, whimpering and blinking in the drizzle.

From within the horde of believers near the bonfire, a bearded man wearing a blacksmith's leather gloves emerged, then crouched and pushed the tip of a metal poker into the base of the bonfire. Milly stifled a scream as she watched. Moments later the tip of the poker was withdrawn red hot and glowing.

Through her tears, Milly whined. 'Please don't. Please don't do this.'

'It has to be done,' Esme said, her voice calm and almost serene. 'You have to be purified. You are tainted and corrupted, but once the pain has passed you will feel joy and relief, and you will be free.'

Milly groaned through clenched teeth. 'Please don't, Esme. You don't have to do this.'

The old woman kissed the top of Milly's head then whispered in her ear. She spoke with affection and the certainty of holy knowledge.

'It's all right to scream, child.'

And then she stepped away while more hands held Milly in place. The people who weren't participating backed away to make space for the man with the burning poker. They all went silent except for a lone woman to Milly's right, who murmured words from a browned and stained book with yellowing pages, and kissed a wooden cross held in one hand.

The man approached with the poker held out before him. He didn't look at Milly. His face dripped with sweat. With his hands shaking gently, he walked behind Milly and halted.

Torchlights from the crowd glared on her face and swept over her swollen stomach, and she bowed her head, feeling sick and terrified and aghast at it all. Something moved inside her, as if uncoiling or blossoming. She listened for a heartbeat accompanying her own, but couldn't hear anything past the streaming of blood through her veins. She sniffled and squirmed, her eyes smarting, feeling as though they were bulging within their sockets.

The children held hands and stared down at her. Psalms were whispered by damp mouths.

'Salvation,' someone said.

The dogs in the kennels began barking.

She felt the heat of the poker near her exposed back and she went rigid, her skin erupting in gooseflesh and cold trembling. She gritted her teeth until a high-pitched ringing filled her ears. Bracing for the first moment of agony. Preparing for the pain. She uttered a small cry and silently begged it to be done so that it could all be over, for now, on this awful day. Just another awful day. She found herself praying to the gods that she half-remembered from her time in the other places, and it held back the babble of frenzied thoughts.

Milly closed her eyes and waited.

The dogs' barking rose into plaintive, fearful howls, which went on for a few moments before they were silenced by the shrill wail of what Milly knew to be the Wraith.

CHAPTER THIRTY-TWO

'What the fuck was that?' one of the men said. No one answered. But Milly knew without doubt, and she opened her eyes when the first screams rose from the back of the crowd.

The Wraith was among them, its tendrils glimpsed in the midst of the panicking crowd, flailing and lashing, busy and swift as they tore people apart. The creature shredded meat with its terrible circular maw. A mutilated body was flung upon the bonfire, and blood and fat burned. The children were screaming and crying, and one of them, a girl, was plucked from the ground by a snaking tendril and snatched away into the dark. A woman wailed, rushed after her, and wasn't seen again.

The blast of a shotgun cut through the screams, but didn't fire again. And then Milly saw the Flayed enter the camp from out of the shadowed tree line and set about the travellers with knives and spiked blades. They butchered men, women and children. They were merciless things, their skinless faces revealed in the light of the bonfire, zealots and maniacs with grinning lipless mouths and rabid eyes. Some of them loped on all fours, sniffing the air like hunting animals savouring the musk of their prey.

Esme shrieked. The men's hands loosened on Milly, allowing her to look back at the old woman as she was skewered through the stomach by one of the Wraith's sharp limbs. She was lifted from the ground, her hands clasping and pawing at the tendril, her face shocked, gasping and agonised, until another appendage wrapped around her throat and began squeezing. There was the sound of wet tearing, and the tendril gently plucked her head from her shoulders. Blood fountained from the stump of her neck, spraying Milly and the men, and then Esme's head and her body were discarded like a broken toy and dropped to the ground, where they landed with meaty thuds.

Milly turned away, struggling to escape before the Wraith came after her, but then there was a flash of swooping movement from a tendril and one of the men holding her fell away all slopping and bisected at his abdomen, intestines tumbling and dripping. He never made a sound as he collapsed into a crumpled wet mess. And with that Milly was released and she dove forward as the other man holding her was snatched by a tendril and pulled screaming into the Wraith's churning mouth. More men with axes and clubs rushed towards the creature. Stray feet kicked at Milly. Blood splattered around her. The death cries of the men forced her to rise and stagger away, clutching her swollen stomach, sick with terror and the writhing inside of her. She was sobbing, inhaling ragged breaths that stung in her chest.

People died around her. People died screaming. Some of the Flayed were laughing. A man with a slashed, gushing throat fell into her and then collapsed at her feet. Some of the caravans were on fire, the flames spreading, rising higher towards the sky, reddening in the darkness of night. The rain fell. She stumbled blindly, flinching from staccato gunshots nearby. She felt the heat of a bullet whip past her face. A wounded man with knife wounds to his stomach begged her for help. A dying child called her the devil.

She saw two Flayed people drag a woman from a caravan and plunge their knives into her back until she stopped screaming. Then they went about carving her up and having a joyous time, murmuring to each other as they worked.

She tripped on a sprawled body and fell to her knees, and before she could rise again a raw hand grabbed her shoulder and pulled her around. The pustule-ridden face of a Flayed man leered down at her. His eyes were alight with euphoria and excitement, bleeding trails of yellowy fluid. His mouth twitched around filed teeth.

'I've got you, now, you little bitch. Doctor Ridings will be so pleased with me.' He spoke as if his gums were swollen. He gripped Milly's left wrist and squeezed. She cried out and struggled, swinging her fist at him, but he blocked her attacks with ease and slapped her across the face. She fell down onto one knee, her face burning, and looked up at him. His body thrummed with a manic energy.

'Little bitch,' he said.

Milly's right hand fell upon the hilt of a knife on the ground. She tightened her fingers around it, without taking her eyes from the man, and swung it upwards and stabbed him in the stomach. The man looked down and regarded the knife as if it were a curious thing that should not have been. Shock widened his eyes.

She pulled the knife free.

The man snarled at her.

She stabbed him again repeatedly until he let go of her and stepped back. His legs gave out and he crumpled, fell onto his side.

Milly looked at her bloodied hand and the dripping blade. She dropped the knife. The man reached for her as she turned away and fled.

And then she halted.

Out of the chaos and murder, her father emerged and stood in her way, his face wan and pained. His eyes damp and regretful.

'Dad,' she said.

'Milly,' he said, noticing her stomach. His voice had lost its strength and hardly seemed like his own. 'It's going to be all right. I'll never leave you again.'

Tears brimmed in Milly's eyes. She took a step towards him then stopped, because something wasn't quite right about Dad's face. She looked at him, the sound of slaughter distant to her. She didn't move.

Dad offered his hand to her.

She stepped back. She imagined that something was inside Dad's body, staring out at her through his eyes. Inhabiting him like a malignant parasite.

'Is it you?' Milly asked.

'Of course it is.' He smiled, and it was almost enough to fool her.

She shook her head.

His eyes hardened, his mouth opened, and he was already lunging to grab her when a wave of intense heat and roaring noise blasted at her back. She was thrown into the air as the world tumbled and screamed and fell into the sky, and then she hit the ground and knew nothing more.

CHAPTER THIRTY-THREE

Albie was awoken by the barrel of a shotgun pressed against his forehead. He lay on his back, disorientated, half-concussed and unable to gather any spit in his mouth. Pain burned throughout him and brought cries rising from his throat. Fragmented memories reared and fell in his mind. His right eye smarted at the shifting sky overhead and the glaring glimpses of the sun.

The man with the shotgun was streaked with dirt, and his clothes were blackened and charred in places. He was shivering, nursing a black eye.

Albie coughed harshly, and then retched, turning his head to one side to spit out mucus that tasted of ash. Something had changed: he was still infected, but he felt like he wasn't under Ridings' control anymore. The connection to the man was gone. The strings had been cut, or at least tangled. But the taint of corruption inside him made him feel sick, although there was nothing in his stomach to purge.

He had lost Milly again. He had allowed her to be snatched away. Again.

The urge to scratch at his face, to peel away the skin, to cut his arms, was almost overwhelming.

The man stepped back. 'Get up. You're not one of us. Get the fuck up, arsehole.'

Albie tried to raise himself from the ground, but only managed to sit slumped and crumpled. Everything swayed around him. He put his hands to his face and felt patches of skin all sore and weeping with lesions. His left eye was swollen shut. His hair was singed. He was trembling with pain. Around him the campsite was a blackened ruin. The bodies of dead travellers were laid out in a line on the ground. He didn't look at them for too long, because of the children there. Blackened, crisped, twisted bodies, some in pieces and broken bits. Some of them were unrecognisable. Dead dogs were arranged in a pile. No sign of the Flayed, and he wondered if they retrieved their dead or if their bodies simply dissipated like smoke.

The bonfire had burned out, leaving only a mound of ash and charcoal. The white of bone in the ashen remains. Blood had dried to black in the patchy grass and dirt. No sign of Milly amongst the few survivors that milled about or sat on the ground shocked and exhausted.

The air smelled of smoke and charred meat. His mouth watered.

'Oh Jesus,' Albie whispered. He wished for rain to wash it all away.

'I told you to get up,' the man said.

With blinding pain that almost finished him, Albie rose to his feet. He tottered, rubbing his tender head and not looking at the shotgun barrel pointed less than a yard from his face.

'Who are you?' the man demanded, his thin face screwed into a sneer.

'I'm no one,' Albie said, instinctively raising his hands.

'You were with those freaks, weren't you? You were with them! That demon killed so many of my people. I saw the man in the bronze mask, too. He was the Devil, I think. After the gas canisters exploded I saw him grab that girl and escape with the other freaks. I went to chase them down, but they fucking vanished.'

Albie sagged, shook his head. The man was going to kill him and that would be that. And he didn't blame him, not at all. He had already forgiven him.

'I deserve revenge,' the man said. 'The demon killed my wife. Tore her into pieces. It fucking ate her while I watched. I want my fucking revenge!'

'I'm sorry,' muttered Albie, and he kept repeating it until the man jabbed the side of his face with the shotgun. Albie stepped back, breathing hard, feeling all the years of grief and guilt gather inside him. He squeezed his eyes shut. He couldn't scream or cry. Bad memories screamed in the red chambers of his mind. He remembered a little about the days after Ridings had infected him: eating scraps from bins with the Flayed; shitting in ditches; drinking stagnant water and praising the black gods of oblivion.

He remembered the night before.

He'd been doing Ridings' work.

And now he had to set things right.

When he felt the rain begin to fall upon him, Albie opened his eyes and looked at the man, who was barely keeping the shotgun steady in his shaking hands; he was blinking away tears, his mouth twitching and trembling, and seemed ready to fall down.

'I'm sorry,' Albie said.

The man raised and fired the shotgun just as Albie reached him and wrenched the barrels aside. Buckshot glanced against the left side of his stomach. The roar of it half-deafened him, but he barely slowed and grabbed the shotgun from the man's hands. The man staggered back, tripped and fell onto his backside, panting in the mud. He looked up at Albie with eyes full of fear, and Albie felt sorry for him, felt sympathy for him, because they were both grieving humans in a terrible, beautiful world.

Albie stood over the man. 'Do you have any spare shells?'

The man nodded, reached into one pocket of his trousers and pulled out a handful of cartridges. Albie reached down and took them.

'I'm sorry for everything that's happened,' Albie said. 'I truly am.'

The man didn't reply, just looked at him. There was no understanding between them.

Albie turned and walked away.

XXXIV

CHAPTER THIRTY-FOUR

He stole a car from the travellers' camp and took to the backroads in the heavy rain. Some remnant of his infection told him where to go, and which roads to take, to reach Ridings and Milly in a place called the Red Cathedral.

The downpour was relentless. The shadows of the rain filled the car. He switched on the headlights. The windscreen wipers worked at full speed, scraping and squealing across the glass. He thought he heard thunder, but it could have been something else.

Once, when sheet lightning blinked in the sky, it revealed something immense, quadrupedal, and long-legged on the horizon. When he looked again it had gone, and there were just the silhouettes of towns and villages.

Other cars passed him, headlights flaring in the rain, their tyres cleaving through standing water and smearing mud that seeped from adjacent fields.

Hatred and revenge and love sustained him, dulled the agony of his body, and focused his mind. He thought he was dying by degrees, slowly fading, but with clarity of vision. He'd found a hoodie and a jumper in the car, and wore the hoodie to obscure most of his face from other drivers and anyone who happened to see him pass by. He'd tied the jumper around his stomach to staunch the slow bleeding in his left side, but it was already damp with his blood and the smell was awful. He stank of approaching death.

From his good eye he wept for the end of his life; his personal apocalypse and the fear of dying alone.

The shotgun was in the boot of the car. If the police stopped him, for whatever reason, and searched the vehicle, he'd deal with them.

He continued onwards as the hours passed and the sky darkened towards dusk.

X

The villagers of Penbrook stood at the roadsides and watched the car as it passed. A group of huddled choirboys, malformed and monstrous in their filthy gowns, grinned at him before turning their pallid faces towards the sky.

Slumping, indistinct and forlorn figures in the rain and the dimming light, marking the way for him on his black pilgrimage, keeping him company on the final approach.

X

It was almost dark when he reached the thin and barren place beyond the cities, towns and villages of his own reality. The wasteland was blackened, a place out of time, existing between worlds.

He stopped the car and turned off the engine, listened to the rain.

Immense and jagged, alien-like in its structure, the Red Cathedral rose from the middle distance and awaited him.

His breath caught in his throat. He winced from his continued agonies. In the car's glove compartment he found a torch and checked it was working before he dropped it into the slack pocket of his hoodie. Then he took a moment, prepared himself, tried to slow his ragged breathing as he clenched his hands together and gave a prayer to any god that was listening. If anything was listening at all.

He sloped out of the car, gritting his teeth, hunched in the rain, opened the back door on his side and pulled out the shotgun. He checked it was loaded then felt the spare shells in his pocket. There was little chance he'd get to use them all.

And he stood for a short while in the rain below the grey sky, the shotgun in his arms, his head lowered as he muttered the names of his family.

Beyond him, terrible things cried and wailed to herald the birth of a monster from a girl's womb.

X X X V

CHAPTER THIRTY-FIVE

Wasteland and vague fields shrouded in rain and fog. Bones in the muddy dirt. The leathery remains of a man grimaced at him from an uncovered grave.

Albie turned away and did not look back.

He dodged blackened arms that rose from the ground to grasp at him. Scarlet toadstools pulsated around his feet. He glimpsed scores of jellyfish-like creatures drifting in the fog clouds. Vague, alien shapes. The rumbling groan of movement deep within the ground. Something screeched in the distance. This thin place stank of corruption and suppurating wounds, of gangrene and spoiled meat. It was thick enough to taste in his mouth.

He limped and coughed, wheezed and whimpered, saying the special names he carried in his heart, until he reached the Red Cathedral and halted before the fleshy doors that offered him entrance. White hot pain flared within the wounds in his side. He raised his head and looked up at the spread of the unearthly structure. It had to be over two hundred feet tall, and half of that wide, appearing like jagged formations of spiked rock. And in places the cathedral was covered in a gnarled and glistening skin. The rain dripped in outer alcoves and recesses that were made of something like meat. The smell, all rotten and dank, brought tears to his eyes and had him hunched over and coughing. Then he straightened, raised the shotgun and made for the doors.

X

Albie pushed the doors open and entered the Red Cathedral, dragging his feet like an ailing beggar in his filthy clothes. He kept the shotgun raised, despite the exhaustion of his arms and the aching in his bones. Rain dripped from him to the stone floor. He stood in a cavernous space, the ceiling high enough to be obscured in darkness. Shadows congealed and reared like belligerent spirits. The walls breathed. Beads of sweat rose on his skin from the humid air. A terrible smell of offal, a taint of butchery and slaughterhouses. He thought the cathedral was alive and tried not to consider it again. There was madness in the air, mixed with pestilence and fungal decay. He imagined himself inhaling microscopic spores that would take hold in his lungs and bloom with cancerous tendrils.

Ten metres ahead of him, a large opening in the floor descended into the darkness, and from it came Milly's screams and cries of pain. Albie shuddered, his heart aching with rage. A red urge broiled inside him, made him murderous and close to hysteria.

He swept the shotgun over the walls as he moved, watching for threats from the shadows, but wondered if the weapon would be any use against the terrible things that waited for him.

He stood at the edge of the opening. The floor sloped down into nothingness. The base of his stomach fell away as he breathed harshly, flinching each time Milly screamed from far away. His hands gripped the shotgun tightly, whitening his knuckles until they were numb, and it took all of his nerve to walk into that sheer darkness of oblivion.

X

He found a maze of dim, serpentine tunnels and corridors where the walls were flesh and pulsed wetly. He walked on, directionless, trying to follow Milly's cries. He switched on the torch and held it alongside the shotgun as he moved slowly along the damp floor. The stink of the air was cloying, grainy, choking, and stung his eyes. Pale worms writhed around his feet.

After a long while in the tunnels, he halted when he heard the scraping of movement behind him, getting closer.

He turned around and the torchlight revealed the squirming, thrashing form of the Wraith. It filled the tunnel. Its serrated maw gnashed in anticipation

Albie fired twice, emptying the shotgun. The recoil pushed him back, his feet skidding on the floor. The Wraith squealed as it fled down a side tunnel, tendrils scratching against the walls. Albie wasn't even aware he'd been holding his breath until he exhaled sharply.

Despite his shaking hands, he quickly reloaded the shotgun, glancing about and waiting for the creature to reappear, and then he turned back around and started down the tunnel again. His steps were slow and hesitant in the dripping of the darkened tunnels. He lost track of time, the seconds marked by the punctuation of his daughter's screams from afar. And he was slowing, parts of him failing, blood loss making him woozy and weak.

He told Milly he was on his way and he'd be with her soon.

X

The Wraith came for him again in those shadowed and stinking tunnels, this time from above after clambering down an overhead shaft. Its tendrils flailed and whipped, and one coiled around his left ankle and pulled him to the floor. As he was slammed down on his back, he dropped the torch but held on to the shotgun, knowing that if he let it go he'd be dead.

The torch came to rest on the floor and in its light the Wraith swayed and wailed – the sounds like knives inside Albie's skull. Its multiple eyes amidst the riot of surrounding tendrils glowed spectral-white and cold as it dragged him towards its salivating mouth.

With one hand, he swung the shotgun towards the creature and pulled the trigger. The blast was deafening in the cramped space, dulling Albie's hearing. Then the Wraith was shrieking. In its momentary pain it released him, but as soon as he climbed to his hands and knees the tendrils swiped at him, slashing across his back. He screamed and dropped face down, the shotgun slipping from his hand. The Wraith grabbed him again and flung him against the wall. Juddering impact. Something cracked inside him. Blinding pain disorientated him in the shadows and light.

The monster loomed over him. He looked up just as it fell upon him and wrapped its tendrils around his legs and torso, squeezing his ribs against his lungs. His heart faltered and he couldn't breathe. The Wraith hauled him against the wall and regarded his struggling body with the nest of bulbous eyes at the centre of its mass. It stank of brine and rotting seafood. It hissed and wheezed through its circular mouth, which then began to open in preparation of its meal, exposing the glistening pinkish lining within.

Albie stared into the glowing eyes of the monster. This was it. That moment before death. But there was no fear, just a fleeting hope that he'd see his family again in some other place, mixed with regret and disappointment for not saving his daughter. His Milly. His blood. The heart of his heart.

'Not yet,' he said; a whisper only he could hear. And within him something awoke and filled him with raw anger that swelled in his heart and had him screaming the breath out of his lungs. It was if he was watching from above as he pulled himself towards the Wraith and began clawing frantically at its eyes with his rigid hands.

The creature squealed and thrashed, slashing at Albie with its tendrils; but he was caught in delirium and rage and only after he used his teeth did he relent and allow the Wraith to blindly skitter away and collapse against the wall.

Covered in the Wraith's eye-fluids and blood, Albie rose to his knees, gasping for breath, holding his hands at his face. He tasted the awful creature in his mouth. When his breathing slowed and the red veil had faded, he stood and looked at the creature and felt a small amount of pity for it, because it was merely an animal bred to hunt and kill for its master, and nothing more.

Trembling, half-blind, and muttering to himself, he picked up the shotgun and checked that it was loaded then took a step towards the Wraith. The beast was flailing weakly, wheezing laboured breaths, its horrid mouth sagging open. Where its eyes had been there was merely ragged, jellied flesh and torn muscle that glistened in the torchlight. It turned towards Albie and shrieked one last time, before he levelled the shotgun and released the dying animal from its obligations.

The blast echoed on through the tunnels and warned of the father's approach.

CHAPTER THIRTY-SIX

He went on, exhausted and hopeful, bedraggled and sagging from his wounds. Every step was pain. Shadows moved around him, withdrew then came forward again, and he pawed them away with his weak arms and slashed hands.

In some place away from him, Milly seemed to never stop crying, and when she screamed it broke things within his ailing body and blackened his heart.

He went on.

X

The ceiling of the tunnel widened and rose higher until it vanished high above him. Milly's cries sounded louder.

Closer, he thought. Closer. She was nearby. He risked a smile that was mostly madness and forlorn hope.

The screams stopped.

He rushed onwards with all his strength, punishing his agonised body. Panic whitened his vision, pushed him beyond desperation. Time passed in fragments in that humid hell. He lost himself. He blacked out, came to, and sobbed as he hurried through tunnels that all looked identical and were littered with small bones.

At last, out of the confusion, he found himself at the entrance to a circular room, and in the middle of the floor Ridings and the hunched forms of the Flayed stood with their backs to him, oblivious to his arrival. Two Coleman lanterns glowed on the floor, giving light to the centre of the room.

Albie stopped, leaning against a damp wall that shivered against him, and slowly regained his breath. He wiped his good eye with the back of his wrist. The itching soreness of his burnt skin was maddening.

He saw her, out there with the creatures. He whispered her name. She'd been restrained to an antiquated hospital gurney, her legs splayed and held in place with knots of rope. She was unmoving, pallid, her eyes closed. She wore a white gown that brought to Albie images of sacrificial victims and offerings of blood at harvest time. He restrained a sob, his breath shuddering in his chest, and started towards them with the shotgun raised.

The Flayed turned around and watched him approach. They did nothing but grimace through their lipless mouths. They said nothing. Their numbers were less than before.

'Ridings,' he said, and halted several steps away from the man and his acolytes.

Doctor Ridings pivoted slowly and appraised Albie through the eye holes in his mask. Against his chest, he cradled a small form in a red blanket.

It was a baby.

'Milly's baby,' Albie said, and it was as if his insides had tumbled out.

Ridings nodded. Glanced down at the squirming shape he held. A tiny hand, pale and withered, marbled with black veins, rose from the blanket wrapped around it and reached towards Ridings' face, thin fingers flexing and twitching. The baby made noises of squirming damp and gurgling. It barely sounded human.

'And here you are, Infidel,' said Ridings. 'You only missed the birth by minutes.' The man tutted. 'I see that the infection did not fully take with you. These things happen, I suppose. It matters very little now.'

Albie said nothing.

Ridings made an amused sound. 'Do you want to see this beautiful boy's face? It is a privilege to look upon him. But I can't promise you'll be the same afterwards.'

Albie kept the shotgun pointed at Ridings. 'Is Milly dead?'

'You can see to her,' said Ridings. 'I have no need for her, now the boy is born. She has done what was asked of her. You should be proud, Infidel. Be proud of her and what she has given to the world, given to all of us, because soon, Infidel, things will be coming through the thin places. My son will bring them into our world. Gods and monsters and all the other beasts. There will be an emergence. Worlds will collide. Reality will change. This boy will lead the way and there will be suffering and joyful chaos.'

Albie took a step forward. 'I said I was going to kill you.'

Ridings snorted, made no attempt to back away. 'Yes, you promised. I remember. But now I hold your grandson, Infidel. That changes things. He is of your blood. You would not kill an innocent child.'

Down the barrels of the shotgun Albie looked at Ridings then the newborn, blinking sweat from his eye. His other, wounded eye offered nothing. Palpitations in his heart. Pulse choking in his throat.

His finger tightened on the trigger, but Milly's voice stopped him before the shotgun fired.

'Dad, let them go.' Her pained face, wet with tears, was turned towards him. She winced with each breath. Such a slight thing. Just a little girl.

'What?' he said.

'Let them go. Please. It's my son and I don't want him to die. I don't want anyone else to die. I just want to go home, Dad. Will you take me home?'

Sick with exhaustion, Albie slumped, faltered, swaying on his feet. But he didn't lower the shotgun.

Ridings said, 'We're leaving, now. You will never see us again, I promise. Take your daughter, your beloved, and take her back to the world you know.'

Milly was crying. Crying for him.

Albie cursed God with all his will and strength, then lowered the shotgun and stood there in the silence of the red cathedral.

CHAPTER THIRTY-SEVEN

Ridings had fled with the newborn and the rest of the Flayed, vanishing into the dark in a solemn procession.

Alone in the great room, he untied Milly from the gurney and lifted her into his arms and held her tenderly. He ignored the pain that flared in his limbs. He was afraid of breaking parts of her that were yet unbroken. She was more fragile than ever, whimpering and crying, her face bloodless and her eyes hooded with exhaustion. The insides of her legs were wet with blood. He kissed her on the cheek. She looked at his face and said she was sorry for all that had happened. She said she was sorry that he'd been hurt. Then she closed her eyes and slackened in his arms, and when Albie felt for her pulse there was nothing.

'No,' he whispered, shaking his head in denial. The ruin of his face creased with grief. 'No, don't leave me, Milly. Please don't leave me.'

In the shadows at the edges of the birthing room, thin shapes emerged with twitching appendages upon the wrinkled skin of their naked, bipedal bodies. Pinkish eyes squinted at the light of the lanterns. Hairless heads bobbed and ducked, bird-like in their movements. Arachnid faces glistening and seeping. Something on all fours that looked like a skinless dog sucked in a shuddering breath and raised its head towards Albie. Its eyes were gone.

And behind the creatures, other things of long limbs and elongated abdomens unfurled from the dark and dragged themselves into the light.

Gods and monsters drawn to this world.

Albie kept hold of his daughter and fled the birthing room.

X

The escape through the tunnels was taken in sheer panic and terror, and it was only with blind luck that he found the way out.

Up the slope he went, digging his heels in, and then through the opening to the chamber at ground level. Milly was cold, unresponsive to Albie's pleas to open her eyes.

He staggered through the Red Cathedral's doors and emerged into heavy rain and the failing light of dusk. He looked ahead, terrified that the car would be gone, but it was still where he'd left it. He hurried through the rain. When he reached the car, he laid Milly across the backseat then climbed behind the steering wheel and turned the keys and started the engine.

He looked towards the Red Cathedral and saw that it was gone, lost in the rain, as if it had never been there in the first place.

X

It was full dark when they arrived at the small hospital on the edge of some unknown town. He abandoned the car outside the main entrance and carried Milly through the sliding doors and into the reception and the waiting room where ill and injured people waiting to be seen turned in their seats and gawped at the shambling figure that carried a dead girl.

He cried out in wordless agony and fell to his knees under the glare of bleached lights. He begged for help while nurses and attendants clamoured around him. Milly was lifted from his arms and placed on a gurney. A security guard watched from nearby. Two nurses with concerned faces helped him to a chair and sat him down. He watched as Milly was wheeled away down the corridor with people alongside her.

They disappeared beyond a set of doors and into sterile white corridors.

Albie sagged in his chair. People stared at him. The nurses knelt by him, asking his name, asking questions that he couldn't answer. All he could do was watch the doors through which Milly had gone, and wait for her to return.

CHAPTER THIRTY-EIGHT

Short fragments of consciousness were all he knew in the hospital bed in the plain room that smelled faintly of cleaning chemicals. Glimpses and images of medical staff standing around his bed. A soft flap of a white coat and the tapping of a pencil on the clipboard kept at the end of his bed. Garbled voices from beyond his room.

The police arrived soon after, and asked him questions, but whenever he tried to answer he would pass out and fall into bad dreams. His nightmares were of squealing infants wrapped in red cloth.

The beeping of a monitor kept pace with his slow breathing. A drip kept him hydrated. Most of his body was wrapped in bandages and dressings, and medication numbed the pain and softened his bones.

A detective in a cheap suit sat at his bedside and read a newspaper. Albie tried to see the date on the front page, but his vision was watery and flickering.

Injections in his arms. Examinations and procedures. A doctor shone a light in his good eye. A nurse smiled down at him.

On one unknown day, when he heard rain against the window, Kathleen appeared at the foot of his bed and stared at him, her face sad and wan. She went away at some point, but Albie wasn't sure when, and he thought he could smell her old perfume for a long while afterwards.

X

More short periods of knowing, and then a fever and sudden fits that left him wishing he was dead. His thoughts were in disarray, incoherent and muddled.

There were faint screams from deeper in the hospital, and running footfalls in the corridor outside his room. A metallic banging that rose and fell in volume. Scratching in the walls. The keening of an animal. He thought it was all imagined, concocted by his mind as it sampled and indexed the terrors he'd experienced.

He spent one entire night in darkness, his cries unanswered by any nurse or passer-by. No doctors came to visit. No assistance offered in the dark hours. He lay there weeping, and when the morning light arrived all was silent beyond his room.

X

He woke to find Milly sat in the chair at his bedside. She was watching him, a hopeful smile on her face. She wore a white dressing gown. Her frail appearance broke his heart.

'Milly,' he rasped.

'It's OK, Dad,' she said. 'It's OK. They saved me, but I couldn't save them. I couldn't save any of them. How are you feeling?'

'I'll live.' Slowly he sat up, wincing as his joints scraped together and thin bones creaked. The smalls wound in his left side stung. His mouth was dry and tasted of medicine. He touched the creased dressings on his face. 'What happened? I thought you were dead.'

Milly's smile faded. 'Let's go for a walk.'

She rose and helped her father from the bed, disconnecting the tubes and wires from him. He was in a papery gown and smelled of stale sweat. He pulled on a bathrobe and hospital-issue slippers then took his daughter's hand and they left the room.

EPILOGUE

They walked through the deserted wards and corridors of the hospital, past empty beds and vacant work-stations. Medical equipment, discarded clothes and loose sheets of paper littered the floor, with overturned gurneys, wheelchairs and trolleys. All of it abandoned and left behind. Not a patient or staff member to be seen. There weren't even any bodies.

The oppressive silence hurt Albie's ears.

Their footfalls echoed on ahead of them, down murky corridors.

'What happened to everyone?' he said.

'They went away.'

'Where did they go?'

'They won't be coming back. It's all changed now. It's a new world, Dad. There is a new order to things and we must accept it, because there's nothing else to be done.'

Albie looked around, then turned and regarded his daughter and clasped her hand with both of his own. 'We'll be all right. Whatever happens, we'll be all right.'

They walked to the front of the hospital and emerged from the doorway into watery daylight and stood at the top edge of the car park. Milly didn't let go of his hand.

The sky was mostly grey, with flashes of the sun past the shifting clouds. The car park was empty except for some scattered gurneys and a red Range Rover skewed across two parking spaces. Trash skittered across the tarmac in the breeze. Leading away from the car park, the access road was lined with wilting, blackened trees, and beyond that was a street where nothing moved and dappled sunlight filled the windows of houses. Something large had passed through the street and trampled the cars at the roadsides.

A helicopter droned high overhead then faded away to the east.

'Where should we go?' Albie said.

Milly tightened her grip on his hand, looked up at him, and offered a frail smile. 'I don't think it matters, Dad.'

'Yeah, you're right. It doesn't matter.'

'Let's go, Dad.'

'Okay. Let's go.'

They went out into the new world, father and daughter together, never to be separated again.

ABOUT THE AUTHOR

Rich Hawkins hails from deep in the West Country of England, where a childhood of science fiction and horror films set him on the path to writing his own stories. He credits his love of horror and all things weird to his first viewing of John Carpenter's THE THING when, aged twelve, he crept downstairs late one night to watch it on television.

His debut novel THE LAST PLAGUE was nominated for a British Fantasy Award in 2015.

He currently lives in Somerset with his wife, their daughter and their dogs. They keep him sane. Mostly.

https://www.facebook.com/rich.hawkins.98

http://richhawkinswriter.co.uk/

https://twitter.com/RichHawkins4

Also by Rich Hawkins

KING CARRION

In a town in southern England, people are going missing.

Mason, a homeless ex-con, arrives in the town to beg his wife for a second chance and atone for past mistakes.

A vampire god once worshipped by ancient Britons has awoken from hibernation and plans to turn Great Britain into a vampire isle. But first, people of the town must be converted, and the gospel spread.

Within a week, the town is quarantined by the military, and the nights belong to the undead.

There will be no escape for the survivors…

Also featuring Rich Hawkins

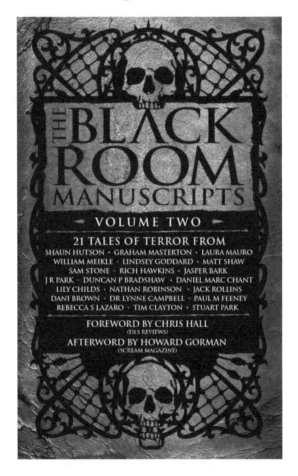

THE BLACK ROOM
MANUSCRIPTS - VOLUME
TWO

Featuring stories by Shaun Hutson, Graham Masterton, Laura Mauro, William Meikle, Lindsey Goddard, Matt Shaw, Sam Stone, Rich Hawkins, Jasper Bark, J R Park, Duncan P Bradshaw, Daniel Marc Chant, Lily Childs, Nathan Robinson, Jack Rollins, Dani Brown, Dr Lynne Campbell, Paul M Feeney, Rebecca S Lazaro, Tim Clayton and Stuart Park.

A foreword by Chris Hall (DLS Reviews) and an afterword by Howard Gorman (Scream magazine).

All profits made from this book will be donated to Alzheimer's Research UK.

.

"The Black Room Manuscripts Volume 2 is a blistering anthology." – Ginger Nuts Of Horror

"A collection of 21 short stories written by a virtual who's who of the UK's indie horror scene." - The Slaughtered Bird

"The Black Room Manuscripts: Volume Two more than just delivers top quality horror fiction – it floods the veins with a concoction so imaginatively varied and versatile that the genre's never looked more alive." – DLS Reviews

The Sinister Horror Company is an independent UK publisher of genre fiction founded by Daniel Marc Chant and J. R. Park. Their mission a simple one – to write, publish and launch innovative and exciting genre fiction by themselves and others.

For further information on the Sinister Horror Company visit:

SinisterHorrorCompany.com
Facebook.com/sinisterhorrorcompany
Twitter @SinisterHC

Lightning Source UK Ltd.
Milton Keynes UK
UKHW01f1457270618
324879UK00001B/6/P

9 781912 578054